FROM THE LIBRARY OF

THE STORY SEEKER

THE
STORY
SEEKER

KRISTIN O'DONNELL TUBB

with illustrations by Iacopo Bruno

A New York Public Library Book

HENRY HOLT AND COMPANY · NEW YORK

Henry Holt and Company, *Publishers since 1866*
Henry Holt® is a registered trademark of Macmillan Publishing Group, LLC
120 Broadway, New York, NY 10271 · mackids.com

ISBN 978-1-250-30109-3

Library of Congress Control Number 2019932418

Our books may be purchased in bulk for promotional, educational, or business use.
Please contact your local bookseller or the Macmillan Corporate and
Premium Sales Department at (800) 221-7945 ext. 5442 or by
email at MacmillanSpecialMarkets@macmillan.com.

First edition, 2020 / Designed by Katie Klimowicz
Printed in the United States of America by Bang Printing,
Brainerd, Minnesota

1 3 5 7 9 10 8 6 4 2

For Helen, my mom,
and Kate, my friend

CONTENTS

THE
STORY
SEEKER

CHAPTER ONE

Medicine,

Dewey Decimal 610

SEE ALSO: *health, diseases*

What's the value of a story? Certainly you can look at the price tagged to a book, see how many dollars it takes to add that book to your collection. But surely a story has far more worth than that? Perhaps a story's value should be measured in pleasantries, not pennies. Knowledge, not nickels. Delights, not dollars.

A story's value isn't determined by money but moments. Moments that take your breath away, that make you giggle, that make you cry. Does a story overwhelm you with grief, flood you with joy, or fill you with dread?

Dread. Sorry to begin our tale with such gloom and doom, Dear Friend, but dread is exactly where *this* story begins.

Viviani Joffre Fedeler sprawled across her quilted bed, clicking her fountain pen against her teeth, pondering her sprawled-open captain's log. (She refused to call it a diary, thank you, even if that's exactly the purpose it served.) Viviani's bedroom looked like any other kid's bedroom in the whole of New York City: messy dresser drawers, peeling wallpaper, discarded candy wrappers, piles of clothes. It was all very normal indeed. Oh, except that Viviani's bedroom was part of an eight-room apartment on the second story of the New York Public Library. Yep, the famous one. With the lions out front.

She tapped her pen nib against the paper to start the flow of ink: *February 21, 1929,* she wrote inside her captain's log. *Dear Friend, . . .*

Things That Are Worse Than Going to the Doctor's Office:

—getting mauled by a tiger (probably)

—subway rats with red eyes that hiss at you

—~~tight knickers~~—Strike that. Going to the doctor is worse.

—That's it. Everything else awful involves going to the doctor.

"Viv, let's go!"

2

Viviani groaned at the sound of her mother's voice and rolled off her bed. Maybe she could hide in the large book return bin on the main floor. Sure, it'd hurt, getting pelted with all those books sliding through the return slot. But it couldn't hurt more than getting a shot. She hated needles. Needles were *the worst*. She plodded into the living room, where her older brothers, John Jr. and Edouard, were waiting with Mama.

Mama pulled a woolen cloche hat over Viviani's ears. She tugged the knot of Edouard's scarf tighter—so tight he pretended to wheeze. Mama smiled and turned her attention to John Jr., the eldest of the Fedeler kids.

"Wet hair?" she asked with a smile, cocking an eyebrow. "In this weather?"

"I'll be fine." John Jr. pounded on his chest. "Healthy as an ox. I'm looking forward to the doc telling me what a fine specimen of a human I am. Unlike these two." He jerked his thumb at Viviani and Edouard. "I'm certain they'll have to stay behind for further medical testing."

Testing. Just the word made Viviani's mouth sour. Why is every form of the word *test* so positively awful?

Mama stood on tiptoe to cram a knitted woolen cap on John Jr.'s head. "You won't be as healthy as an ox when you catch pneumonia."

John scowled. "Aw, Ma!"

Mama clucked him silent. "It might be almost spring,

3

but it's still chilly. Come on. Let's get to Dr. Monroe's office."

The four Fedelers—Mama, John Jr., Edouard, and Viviani—walked out of their cozy apartment, through the empty marble corridors of the New York Public Library, and down the winding staircase.

"Morning, Mr. Green!" Viviani shouted to the custodian mopping in Astor Hall. "Those floors look clean enough to eat off!"

"Don't you dare eat off my floors," Mr. Green grumbled, mop sloshing. Viviani chuckled despite her nerves, and the Fedelers wound their way through the building, toward the delivery docks.

"Hullo, Jack!" Viviani called to the fellow loading boxes of books onto one of the bookmobiles. Her voice echoed in the cavernous tunnel, *hullooo!* Jack straightened and mumbled hello in return, the cigarette in his lips bouncing.

"No smoking in the library, Jack," Mrs. Fedeler yelled over her shoulder. "You know, books and whatnot."

Jack grunted again. Viviani would've laughed except for the impending doom that awaited her at the doctor's office.

The Fedelers walked outdoors and blinked in the sunlight on Fortieth Street before turning right toward the Times Square subway station. On the way down the narrow staircase, Viviani thought she saw a long, disgusting tail.

"Subway rat," she muttered. "Now all I need is to be mauled by a tiger, and this day is officially as bad as it gets." She shivered and continued following her family into the roaring tunnels burrowed beneath the city.

They purchased their subway nickels at the wooden operator booth and went through the turnstile. The subway cars whooshed to a stop before them, and the Fedelers ran to board the train as if they were on a grand adventure, instead of hurtling toward needles and knives. Ads were posted at each stop—"Twenty-Eighth Street!" "Prince!" "Canal!"—and one was for Chicken Dinner, a popular candy bar from the Sperry Candy Company. The thought made Viviani's stomach churn even harder. The car swayed and jerked, lights flickering, all the way south to their stop at the domed City Hall station.

"Mama, why do I have to go to the doctor? I feel perfectly fine," Viviani said as she dragged her feet, reluctantly following her family up and out of the dark tunnels, back into the blinding sunlight.

"You look like a very healthy eleven-year-old, even with that glum face," Mama said, laughing. "But I want a clean bill of health for all three of you, especially with so many illnesses cropping up. Now come along and stop scuffing your shoes, Viviani. They're brand-new."

Mama led them to a building at the corner of Broadway and Fourteenth, up three flights of stairs, and through a door with DR. MONROE, PEDIATRICS stenciled in gold lettering on the window.

The office was long, narrow, and lined with thick, musty, leather-bound books. Also crammed along the walls were desks and metal tables with sharp objects (so sharp!). It smelled like strong chemicals, potent enough to make Viv's nostrils tingle. Her stomach flopped again. She and her siblings drooped into chairs.

"You'll probably have to get a shot, you know," John Jr. whispered to her.

Viv gulped and said with a glare, "You don't know that."

At the waver in her voice, John Jr. leaned over, studying Viviani's face. "Hey, Red! I was just teasing." He put her in a gentle headlock and mussed her curls. "Tell you what. I'll put on a disguise, a red-haired wig and a dress, and I'll take the shot for ya."

Viviani laughed. Edouard offered John Jr. his glasses. "Take mine, too, then?"

Dr. Monroe burst into the room, high heels clacking on the wooden floor. She was about fifty, Viviani guessed, and her lipstick always fanned out in a way that made her seem spidery and stern. Viviani pictured her cooking potions over a large black cauldron in the back

6

room, cackling and singing, *"Double, double toil and trouble . . ."*

A young man, who didn't appear much older than John Jr., shuffled in behind her. He toted an armful of books, and his crooked glasses framed red, tired eyes. He looked like he needed about three solid days of sleep.

"Benjamin," Dr. Monroe barked at him.

He dropped the books onto one of the tables with a *flump*, then turned to her. "Ma'am?"

"It's good to see you again, ah, John Jr.," Dr. Monroe said, nodding at Edouard. "Eddie," she said, pointing at John. "And Vivian."

"Viviani," Viv corrected, but Dr. Monroe had already clacked farther into the room and was pumping Mama's hand in a vigorous handshake. "Mrs. Fedeler. Tell me what's on your mind."

"Well, Doctor, the warmer months are approaching, and I have some questions about the possibility of a polio epidemic in the city."

"Oh, well, what you should be worried about is tuber-culosis. Much, much worse . . ."

Viviani felt light-headed at the word *epidemic*, and her thoughts began racing. All she knew of tuberculosis was that her favorite author, Edgar Allan Poe, lost two loved ones to TB, and he wrote the super-creepy "Masque of the Red Death" because of it. In the story, a character named Prince Prospero tries to hide from a plague known as the Red Death. But his greed gets the best of him, and he hosts a lavish masquerade ball as others perish outside his castle. The prince ultimately realizes you can't hide from death, no matter your wealth. Viviani shuddered.

The young apprentice, Benjamin, approached the kids with a clipboard. He donned a head mirror to reflect light into mouths, ears, and eyes. Benjamin snatched a tongue depressor off a metal table filled with sharp objects (so very sharp!) and positioned the mirror to bounce bright light at John Jr.'s face, seeming distracted even as he poked and prodded.

"So, Edouard," Benjamin said.

"I'm Viviani, actually," John said.

Benjamin sat up, flipped his head mirror aside, and blinked behind his thick glasses. His expression was so bug-like and silly that it actually made Viv's mouth tug upward.

John Jr. gave Benjamin a light punch on the arm. "Just joshing, of course. I'm John. *That's* Viviani," he said, thrusting his thumb toward Edouard.

Edouard waved.

Benjamin tapped his clipboard with his pencil. "It says here John Jr. is the eldest child."

John Jr. nodded.

"So that is you, correct?"

"Two for two, Doc."

"Not a doctor yet, John Jr., just a medical student." Benjamin continued his poking and prodding. "How have you been feeling?"

"Honestly, Doc? Not great. I got a pain *right here*," John Jr. motioned to his whole person. Viviani and Edouard mashed their lips to keep from laughing.

"I see, I see!" Benjamin said, noting this on his clipboard dutifully.

"And, Doc . . ." John Jr. leaned in and whispered, "It kinda hurts when I . . . *you know*."

Benjamin looked at him earnestly, then nodded. "Yes, I believe I do."

Appearing concerned, the apprentice rolled his stool over to Edouard. "And you, son? How are you feeling?"

"My tongue hurts," Edouard said, sticking it out. "Eee? Et awl geen oh sohugh."

"Do you mean your *throat* hurts?"

Edouard shook his head. "No, my *tongue*. Oh, and my toenails. They hurt, too."

"Your toenails?" Benjamin was furiously scribbling this down.

"Yes, sir. All ten."

Benjamin continued poking the boys, and Viviani

9

tried not to giggle as her brothers rattled off symptoms like their eyelashes falling out and their bones popping when they flexed their fingers *just so*, see, Doc?

Finally, Benjamin rolled up to Viviani, who was feeling better, thanks to her brothers' antics. "It's the tip of my nose, sir," she said as earnestly as she could. "It feels numb."

"You mean when you walk in the cold?" Benjamin scrawled on his clipboard.

"No, then it feels like it's on fire!"

Viv's brothers shook with held-in laughter. Benjamin pursed his lips, clearly concerned about this growing list of ailments plaguing the Fedeler children.

"Dr. Monroe!" he shouted over his shoulder, with a rising level of panic in his voice. "You need to come see this!"

Dr. Monroe *clackclackclack*ed toward them, mouth pursed, with Mama following close behind. The doctor looked over the rim of her tiny spectacles and scanned the list of symptoms Benjamin had dutifully recorded.

"Oh," she said. "Hmmm." She touched her fingers to her chest. "Oh, my!"

"This situation seems dire," Benjamin said, but Viviani noticed a twinkle in his eye. Was he playing along? Or was that just a trick of the light? "How should we diagnose this?"

Dr. Monroe nodded, eyeing the Fedeler kids. "I think what we have here is a case of OutdoMySibling-itis. It is extremely contagious, and quite dangerous if left unchecked."

John Jr., Edouard, and Viv suddenly became very interested in the patterned rug running the length of the room.

"I usually prescribe shots for that," Dr. Monroe said, peering sternly over her spectacles. Viviani could *juuust* hear the beginning of a witchy cackle. Her stomach somersaulted.

"Oh, I don't think we need a shot, Doctor, do we?" Benjamin interjected, seeing the look on Viviani's face.

Dr. Monroe leaned closer to the Fedeler trio. "Well, this time I'll let your mother decide if a solid dose of castor oil might do the trick instead."

Castor oil—*ick!* Viviani thought castor oil tasted like motor oil. Probably—she'd never drunk motor oil, of course, but it looked just like the thick, goopy medicine.

Mama crossed her arms, her toe tapping as she read the list of symptoms over Dr. Monroe's shoulder. She furrowed her brow, but Viv could see Mama was trying not to laugh.

"Oh, I think I know just the cure," Mama said. "Let's head back to the library, kids. I have a feeling there are some chores I suddenly need done today. *Now.*"

"Chores? At the library?" Benjamin asked, blinking behind his thick glasses.

"We live there," Viviani said. "My papa's the superintendent." She always ballooned with pride when she told people that. It made her very happy to talk about her library home.

"Really? The big library? With the lions out front?"

"That's the one," Mama said. "The Central Building."

"I do all my research there," Benjamin said, and for the first time, he grinned and lost a bit of his seriousness. "I read constantly to keep up with my classes." He gestured at the table full of medical books. "It's such a beautiful building."

"Well, please do stop by our home and say hello the next time you're there," Mama said, gathering scarves and hats and coats. "Viviani has learned to make a wonderful *basbousa*. And if you're done with these books, the kids here would be happy to help you transport some of them back to the library." Mama thumped the huge books Benjamin had dropped onto the table next to her.

Benjamin's smile flickered. "That would be—uh—yeah. That would be great." He sorted through the texts and handed over five huge books. "Thank you, Mrs. Fedeler."

"That's *Mr.* Fedeler," John Jr. said, and Viviani lightly kicked his shin.

CHAPTER TWO

Children's Games,

Dewey Decimal 790.1

SEE ALSO: *games, indoor games, outdoor games*

"Who's up for a tad bit of mischief?" John Jr. asked once they'd hauled all those way-too-heavy books back to the library. By *foot*, because Dr. Monroe had convinced Mama that taking the subway was a bad idea "in light of the tuberculosis threat." Viviani gladly walked the mile and a half after that, and fortunately, Mama decided hauling the hefty journals the whole way back was enough punishment for their doctor's-office hijinks.

Edouard smirked and swept sweat off his brow. "Mischief? I'm in."

Viviani's eyes gleamed. She was in high spirits since the doctor's visit hadn't resulted in pokes and prods, and she was in the mood for some fun. She knew where this invitation was heading.

"Me. Absolutely me. Give me fifteen minutes to gather the Moppets."

A quarter of an hour later, Viviani stood outside on the front terrace of the library, near the wide stone stairs that climbed up to the iron front doors from Fifth Avenue. Her two best friends, Eva Derian and Merit Mubarak, were beside her, squinting through the bright sunshine.

"Wait, you *steal* it?" Merit was saying. She shook her head and peered at the trio of boys gathered across the patio.

"We'll give it back, of course," said Viviani. "But yes. That's the game. It's called *capture* the flag."

"I don't know about this, Viviani."

If Viviani Fedeler had a dime for every time someone had said those six words to her—*I don't know about this, Viviani*—she'd have enough money to buy that whole collection of Little Orphan Annie comics she'd been eyeing at Woolworth's (and she'd stop getting in trouble with Old Man Winkler for reading them without buying them).

Viviani smiled and leaned against the cold metal base of their flagpole, one of two that were planted in front of the main building of the New York Public Library. She pointed to John Jr., Edouard, and their friend

Carroll Case, who guarded the other flagpole, which Viviani knew was exactly 130 paces away. Viviani knew everything about everything when it came to the library.

"It's simple," Viviani said. "We just have to sneak by the boys without getting tagged and lower their flag." Here, the trio of girls looked up at the pennant the boys guarded: the blue, white, and orange flag of New York City. "When we do, we win!" With her fingernails, Viv tapped the flagpole, and it *ting*ed like a tiny bell. The flagpole base was a deep, rich bronze and very ornate, featuring all sorts of carvings of people and animals and flowers and leaves.

Eva pointed up into the brilliant blue sky at their own forty-eight-star American flag: "Oh, and we have to keep *them* from capturing *our* flag, too."

Merit's eyes narrowed further, and Viviani wasn't sure if the cause was skepticism or sunlight.

"Look, Merit," she said, "there are some serious stakes here. John Jr. and Edouard and I have bet our chores for the next two months on this game. If I lose, I'll have a whole pile of extra stuff to do going into the spring recess."

Eva nodded emphatically.

"But if I *win*? No chores over the recess!" Viviani swept her hand grandly at a group of iridescent pigeons nearby and cried, "Why, I'll be as free as these dear winged creatures!"

Viviani flapped her arms and ran toward them, hoping they would dramatically take flight, lofting into the clouds as high as the surrounding skyscrapers. Instead, the flustered birds fluttered, pooped, and stayed on two feet.

Merit laughed. Viviani loved making her laugh. It wasn't too long ago that Merit was the prickly new girl from Giza, Egypt, and it had taken quite an adventure to cement their friendship. Merit sighed. "Okay. I'll guard our flag. You two capture theirs."

Eva and Viviani flung their arms around Merit, and it was the most natural thing in the world now—these three musketeers sharing a hug. The musketeers, in fact, called themselves the Moppets; they had been given the nickname by a newspaper last fall, after they had captured a stamp thief in the library, and well, the name stuck. (After Viviani insisted it should stick.)

The boys called across the long gray patio, over the heads of the library visitors. "You guys ready?"

"Born ready!" Viviani yelled back.

John Jr. looked at his wristwatch, raised his other hand overhead, and dropped it, yelling, "And . . . *go!*"

Edouard dashed forward first, as usual. He was always the pawn in John Jr.'s masterful games. Eva quickly tagged him, and he froze to a spot about midway between the two flagpoles. Library patrons streamed around him like the Hudson River flows around the Statue of Liberty.

Eva was by far the fastest runner, so she quickly darted to the boys' flagpole. But Carroll Case was ready, leaping from behind a marble bench and tagging her, freezing her just as her fingers brushed the flagpole. "Aw, nuts!" Viviani heard her shout.

As Viviani crept toward the boys' flagpole, her heart raced. She scanned the scene: John Jr. had disappeared. Had she remembered to tell Merit that he sometimes crept down to Fifth Avenue, rounded the corner to Fortieth, and snuck up behind from street level?

She hadn't.

She *couldn't* start spring recess with more chores. Could. Not.

Carroll was keeping a tight watch on the boys' home base, circling their pole with sharp eyes. Eva and Edouard remained frozen. If she could get to Eva, tag her and unfreeze her . . .

"There!" Viviani whispered. She'd spotted John Jr. in the crowd. He'd picked up a discarded copy of the *New York Times* and was pretending to read the newspaper. He sat on a low marble wall next to Leo Astor, one of the famous carved library lions. As he read, John Jr. began inching while sitting. He scooted toward their flagpole, closer, closer . . .

Viviani bobbed and weaved through the thickening library crowd, keeping her eyes glued to John Jr. Finally, she yanked away the newspaper and—"Ha *ha!*"

An old man smoking a pipe glared back at her. "What in the *world* are you doing?"

"Uh, sorry, mister. Here's your . . . uh . . ." She looked at the newspaper crumpled in her fist. "The library has clean copies of the *Times* inside if you need . . . first floor to the left . . ."

"Viviani!" Merit shouted. Viviani spun. Merit hopped up and down with glee, clapping and pointing. "I tagged him! I tagged John!"

Sure enough, Merit had tagged John Jr. He stood frozen, still clutching a portion of newsprint and wearing a scowl to beat all.

"Nice work, teamie!" Viv yelled. Now she just had to sneak past Carroll. But how? He circled the flagpole like a security guard inside the library. Positively hawklike.

"Line up, kids, line up! Let's picnic over here before we go inside!"

One of the library patrons was accompanying a group of a billion tiny, squirming kids to the afternoon story time in the children's room.

"Perfect!" Viviani whispered. She dropped to her knees and crept to the center of their wriggling, scratching, whining group. It wasn't exactly easy to crawl over the slab of marble while wearing a low-waisted dress, but Viviani thought of all the chores she'd gladly hand over to John Jr. and Edouard and endured the pebbles.

Sneaking along inside a group of three- and four-year-olds wasn't pleasant, either. They were sticky, and they liked to poke. "Ow," Viviani whispered as a child tugged on one of her curls. "Don't pinch!" The kids giggled and poked some more.

Slowly, the hive of buzzing kids moved toward the boys' flagpole. Carroll's eyes were still scanning the crowd behind her—he didn't see her at all! Viviani's knee landed squarely on the edge of a marble slab, and pain shot through her leg. She muffled her groan and crept closer, closer . . .

"Kids, everyone put a hand on this flagpole while I get a head count," the teacher instructed. *Yes!* It was like this teacher had been sent from above to liberate Viviani from her chores.

The swarm of kids surrounded the flagpole, providing plenty of cover for Viviani to begin climbing the bronze base, which, luckily, had quite a lot of footholds, thanks to all the ornate carvings and arching swirls and scrolls.

The rope! Viviani gripped the cord that suspended the flag of New York City and pulledpulledpulled as fast as she could. The flag lowered. *Almost . . . almost . . .*

Two clips—*snip! snip!*—and the flag was hers!

She'd done it! For the first time ever, she'd beaten the boys at capture the flag!

Merit and a newly unfrozen Eva jumped up and down, cheering as Viviani wrapped the end of the flag around her shoulders like a cape. "Woooohooooo!" she shouted. The flag flapped behind her as she darted about the terrace. "We did it! We captured the flag! No chores for me for *two whole*—"

"VIVIANI JOFFRE FEDELER."

The voice belonged to one Miss Alice Keats O'Conner, the shrewdest librarian in the whole wide world. Viviani's smile sank as she spun around. Miss O'Conner pushed her glasses up on her sharp nose.

"Viviani, what exactly do you think you're doing with the flag of New York City?"

"Sporting it in victory?" she replied. Carroll Case, just behind her now, spurted a laugh. Viviani wondered if Edouard and John Jr. had made a break for it.

"Viviani, I saw you climbing that flagpole base. Do you know how valuable those bases are? Designed by none other than Mr. Hastings himself, you know. You cannot climb them."

The name Thomas Hastings was quite revered around the New York Public Library, as he was one of the folks who had created it.

"Those bases could support a cow, Miss O'Conner,"

John Jr. said, joining the group now. Viviani's grin at him said a silent *thank you* for not leaving her out to dry with the librarian. His grin back said *Don't mention it.* "I don't think an eleven-year-old could break them," he continued.

"Children." Miss O'Conner sighed. She sighed a lot. If there were a trophy for dramatic breathing, Miss O'Conner would win. She pushed her glasses up on her nose again and said, "There's a lot of deep meaning and symbolism in these sculptures."

"Yeah?" John Jr. said. But Viviani knew that tone. It was his *I'm stalling for time* yeah.

"Oh, my, yes. The four figures on each corner of the sculpture represent Discovery, Conquest, Civilization, and Adventure . . ."

Miss O'Conner went on to talk about the symbolism of each carving: the owls that symbolize wisdom, and the turtles that symbolize time, and the signs of the zodiac carved all around, and and and . . .

Even though Viviani knew all about the carvings, she pretended to be engrossed, in hopes that Miss O'Conner would forget to dole out punishments to the Fedeler kids. While nodding eagerly, Viviani felt Edouard quietly take the flag of New York City off her shoulders. He hoisted it, pull by pull, to the top of the eighty-five-foot pine pole.

"And that, children, is why these flagpole bases are so important." Miss O'Conner gently adjusted her glasses and smiled. Carroll, Merit, and Eva now hung in the background.

"Fact," Edouard said. "You are the most knowledgeable librarian in the whole joint, Miss O."

Miss O'Conner blushed. John Jr. pointed at the mob of nursery-school children now entering the building below, at the Forty-Second Street entrance. "Looks like you'll have quite a crowd at story time today, Miss O'Conner."

"Oh, my! Yes! I'd forgotten all about the St. Cecilia nursery-school children joining us. And I really need to catch up on all those overdue books today, too. Oh, pardon me. Pardon me!" She rushed away.

Viviani folded her arms triumphantly across her chest. "So, which chores would you like to start on, Edouard? The washboard? How about shining the silver for you, John?"

John Jr. and Edouard exchanged glances. "We're not doing those," John Jr. said.

Edouard added, "We just bailed you out, Viv!"

Viviani placed her fists on her hips. "But I won, fair and square!"

"Fact," Edouard said. "The word *square* meant 'fair and honest' in the sixteenth century. To say you won fair and square is to say you won fair and fair. Totally redundant."

Viviani huffed. "*You're* totally redundant!"

John Jr. slung an arm over his sister's shoulder.

"Look, Viv. Think about all the extra chores Papa would've doled out if Miss O'Conner had ratted on you."

Viviani's scowl deepened. "Yeah. True."

"So Ed and I just got you out of that mess. The way I see it, we're all clear here. We took care of your chores."

The boys sauntered away, flustering a group of pigeons that fluttered and pooped.

Viviani shook her head as Eva and Merit joined her. She laughed. "Only my brothers can make winning feel like losing, and losing feel like winning."

CHAPTER THREE

Photographs,
Dewey Decimal 779

SEE ALSO: *documentary photography, photojournalism*

The sun was setting behind the library, casting the white marble building in a slant of honey-colored light. "Let's go look at the picture collection again!" Merit bounced on her toes, eyes sparkling, the golden hoops in her earlobes skipping with glee. "I want to show you what I found last time." Viv and Eva agreed. The trio scrambled inside.

The picture collection on the first floor was housed below the Fedelers' eight-room apartment. The girls breezed through a set of swinging double doors and into the land of black and white.

Big, slick photographs. Small tintype photographs. Crumbling, yellowed old photographs. Glossy and shiny negatives. Scary war photos. Smiling family photos. Animals and buildings and nature, all frozen in time with the click of a shutter and the pop of a flash. You name it, the library's picture collection had an image of it. All photos were cataloged with a typewritten description on the back.

Viviani smiled as Merit walked in and inhaled deeply, as if the magic of the room could be absorbed like the scent of roses. Perhaps to Merit it could. Viviani often did this with books—she smelled them as if breathing in fine perfume or delicious cinnamon.

"Hello again, girls!" Mrs. Coe, the archivist for the picture collection, whispered. "Merit, are you back to take a gander at your new pet?"

Merit glowed. "Yes, ma'am."

"Right this way, then." Mrs. Coe led the Moppets to the Animals category, then to the letter *P.*

Merit dug through a bin of photographs just as Viviani had seen her mother dig through jazz records at the Victrola store. "Aha! Here it is! Viv, Eva—*look.*"

Merit pulled out a yellowing piece of cardstock. Glued to it was a photo of what might be the cuddliest, fuzziest, friendliest-looking poof of an animal Viviani had ever seen. Eva apparently thought so, too; both girls squealed, "Awwwwww!"

Mrs. Coe shushed them. Living in the library, Viviani collected shushes like others might collect rocks or shells. She had pockets and pockets full of them. She could likely create a gust of wind.

"What is it?" Viviani loud-whispered.

Merit flipped over the cardstock and pointed to the description. "It's a giant panda. According to this, it's also called a parti-colored bear."

"That's a bear?" Eva said. "It looks more like a teddy bear than a grizzly!"

"You've never seen a picture of one, either?" Merit asked. Both girls shook their heads.

The three pored over the photograph. The bear's ears and eyes were black. So were its arms and legs. Everything else, white. It appeared to smile right off the glossy paper and into Viviani's heart.

"It looks soft as a cloud," Eva whispered.

"It looks like whipping cream," Merit added.

"It wants to come to live with me in the library and star on Broadway and be our best chum," Viviani said. The Moppets giggled.

The girls studied the panda's friendly face, the leafy stalk it clutched, the lush vegetation around it. The description on the back said the first recorded sighting of these bears was in a remote part of China in 1869, and that the plant it was eating was called bamboo. Viviani reached out a finger to stroke its fur, half expecting the slick photo to feel warm and fuzzy.

"Don't touch, Viviani," Mrs. Coe said without even looking up. How do librarians *do* that? "Those photos are rare. Scholars come from all over the world to find a

27

picture of something they've never seen before. So, no fingerprints."

What a miraculous thing photographs were! Here was Viviani Fedeler, eleven-year-old story collector, sitting in a room in New York City, looking at a bear munching bamboo halfway around the globe. This room was full of the same brand of magic: famous temples and exotic plants and wild landscapes, all collected here for people to come and study. Mrs. Coe always said it was the only room of its kind in the whole world. If you wished to know what something looked like and you couldn't get *there*, you came *here*.

"Can you imagine trying to describe a panda bear to someone who'd never seen this picture?" said Viviani, who strove (and often struggled) to find the exact right words. "Where would you even begin?"

"Its black-and-white fur," Merit said right away.

"Its roly-poliness," Eva added.

Viviani nodded, but said, "Still. I wouldn't imagine *this*. There couldn't possibly be an animal more difficult to describe."

Merit smiled. "Oh, wait till you see an aardvark!"

Merit, Eva, and Viviani roly-polied out of the picture collection, pawing and smiling at one another in their best panda imitations. Then they heard it—the jangle of keys!

Merit and Eva knew what to do: *hide!* It was part of an ongoing game known in the Fedeler family as Master Thief. Viviani and her brothers could, on most nights, maneuver throughout the library without once seeing jolly old Mr. Eames, the night security guard. And each day they managed to avoid him, he awarded them ten points toward their Master Thief tally. But a "gotcha!" from Mr. Eames set that Fedeler kid back five points for the day. Viviani was currently in the lead, and she intended to keep it that way.

The girls were in the wide marble hallway at the far end of the first floor, so their best chance at staying out of sight was to quickly duck into the women's restroom. They rushed in through the heavy swinging oak door, and the trio piled into a single stall, giggling. They locked the wooden stall door behind them.

"Surely he won't come in *here*, right, Viv?"

Viviani shrugged and whispered, "Don't know."

When the door swung open, the three girls clambered atop the toilet so their feet wouldn't show below the stall door. They contained their giggling about as well as a cricket contains its chirruping. The Moppets wobbled, bracing themselves against the stall walls, and held on to one another for support.

Clack. Clack. Clack. Someone's footfalls—Mr. Eames's?—slapped the cool, wide tiles lining the women's room floor. They came closer, closer . . . then stopped, right outside their stall. For a moment, Viviani thought of the ghost she'd been told lived in the library. The ghost whom everyone called Big Red. But *nah.* That was just one of the millions of stories in this library, wasn't it?

There was a pause. A *long* pause. The girls held their breath.

Clack. Clack. Clack. The shoes turned and walked back toward the door. Just as it swung open—

Viviani swayed. She grasped for Eva but didn't want to topple her, too, so—

SPLASH!

Viviani's brand-new Mary Jane shoe dunked right into the cold, clear toilet water.

Merit's and Eva's eyes widened. Then they both crammed fists against lips to keep from bursting apart with laughter.

"Your ma's looking for you, Viviani," Mr. Eames said, his voice echoing around the cavernous restroom. "Says you need to head back to the apartment. Something about climbing the flagpole?"

Ugh. Facing Mama with a sopping-wet shoe *and* getting what was sure to be an earful? "I'll send for my pajamas. I believe I'd rather just stay here all night."

CHAPTER FOUR

Creative Writing,

Dewey Decimal 808

SEE ALSO: *authorship, composition and exercises*

Some days, Dear Friend, it feels perfectly criminal to spend time indoors. You know those days: sky so swollen with blue it feels like it might burst, air so crisp it feels like a sip of water, sun so bright even the shadows dance. *That* was the day following Viviani's dunked shoe, and yet Viviani sat indoors at her wooden desk, chin in hand, gazing out the third-floor window to the school-yard below. Spring recess felt oh-so-far away, and the break itself would never be enough time. Then again, Viviani Fedeler felt there was *never* enough time to do all she wanted to do, taste all she wanted to taste, hear and see and smell all she wanted to hear and see and smell.

Miss Hutch circled the room, admiring everyone's

penmanship practice. Viviani snapped back to attention and returned to writing big, swoopy cursive letters:

$$\mathcal{Pp} \;\; \mathcal{Pp} \;\; \mathcal{Pp} \;\; \mathcal{Pp} \;\; \mathcal{Pp} \;\; \mathcal{Pp} \;\; \mathcal{Pp} \;\; \mathcal{Pp} \;\; \mathcal{Pp} \;\; \mathcal{Pp} \;\; \mathcal{Pp} \;\; \mathcal{Pp} \;\; \mathcal{Pp} \;\; \mathcal{Pp} \;\; \mathcal{Pp} \;\; \mathcal{Pp} \;\; \mathcal{Pp}$$
$$\mathcal{Pp} \;\; \mathcal{Pp} \;\; \mathcal{Pp} \;\; \mathcal{Pp} \;\; \mathcal{Pp} \;\; \mathcal{Pp} \;\; \mathcal{Pp} \;\; \mathcal{Pp} \;\; \mathcal{Pp} \;\; \mathcal{Pp} \;\; \mathcal{Pp}$$

"Nice, Viviani," Miss Hutch said. The teacher leaned over her desk and circled in red ink a number of places where Viviani's *P*s had grown too tall, where their tails had extended too long. So many red circles. Her *P*s were a mess! *P*s splattered everywhere. A *P* explosion. *P* soup! Viviani's stomach grumbled at the thought of steaming green stew.

"Now, class," Miss Hutch said, suddenly at the front of the room. How much time had Viviani spent daydreaming about lunch?

"I have a special assignment for you over the next few days. A *writing* assignment."

The class groaned and shifted in their chairs. But not Viviani! Her ears pricked, and she sat straight as a ruler.

"I'd like for you each to write a short story"—more groans here, except from Viv, whose face stretched into a wide grin—"on the theme of friendship. And, class, there is a prize!"

The moaning ceased suddenly, like a dissipating ghost.

"Prize?"

"Wow! Nifty!"

33

"What is it, Miss Hutch?"

Miss Hutch was writing something on the blackboard in her perfect penmanship:

The New York Times

Viviani thought her whole person might explode into tiny, joyous Viviani confetti.

The *New York Times*?

Mama read the *Times* every night, and Papa said it was why she was the smartest person he knew. The newspaper employed professional word weavers who spun ideas into phrases, and phrases into stories, and stories into conversations that changed the world.

"The winner of our essay contest will get to visit the offices of our city's world-famous newspaper . . ."

The groans turned into gasps.

Viviani, Merit, and Eva exchanged excited looks. Eighteen whole floors of people seeking the best stories to share, of ideas and illustrations and photographs and advertisements being pressed into newsprint. Pressed into *permanence*. Heck, the *Times* office was more than just a building—the whole of Times Square was named for this newspaper! Miss Hutch waited for the whispers to subside.

". . . *and* the winning essay will be printed in the pages of the *Times* itself!"

Viviani had died and gone to homework heaven.

Having her name, her words, in the *New York Times*? That was every story collector's dream!

Viviani fancied herself a "story collector" and had been writing regularly in her captain's log for several months now. Her papa, who could charm the timepiece off a train conductor with his stories, was always so proud to see her writing her stories down.

"That's my girl!" he'd bellow when she read one of her stories aloud. "Your words are going to make you famous one day."

Viviani thought Once Upon a Time and Happily Ever After were as much a part of her as her dirty fingernails, her scraped knees, her red hair. If she didn't win this contest, her papa would be so disappointed! If she couldn't show that story *collectors* could also be story *tellers*, like Papa, she'd let her whole family down. And she surely couldn't call herself a story collector any longer if she couldn't figure out how to share the tales she'd gathered with others!

She had to win. *Had* to.

Viviani raced home to the library, up the twenty-eight front steps, through Astor Hall ("Slow it down, Viviani!"), up the staircase, into the apartment, down the long hallway, into her bedroom, and plopped onto her bed.

"Hello, Viviani!" her mother yelled after her.

"Hi, Mama!" she yelled back. She dug through her bedside table drawer.

Her captain's log! She had *dozens* of stories in there about friendship! She'd pick one of those, copy it, enhance it a bit, and *BAM*! Soon her essay would appear in the *New York Times*. And then surely more stories would follow! She could see the headlines now:

SCANDALOUS CRIME RING UNCOVERED!
BY VIVIANI J. FEDELER
THE BEST BROADWAY SHOWS OF THE 1920S
BY VIVIANI J. FEDELER
AMELIA EARHART: AN EXCLUSIVE INTERVIEW
BY VIVIANI J. FEDELER

Viviani flipped flipped flipped through her captain's log, placing a big inky star on all the entries that might be good examples of friendship:

January 14, 1929

Dear Friend,

Today, Merit taught me and Eva some things about photography. She showed us all about shutter speeds and stops, and it got all jumbled in my head. But oh, Merit's photographs! We sometimes develop them in the Printing Office in the library basement (thank you, Mr. Tuttle!). Merit's latest photos included a delicate spider-web dripping with dew. The iced-over fountain in Bryant Park. A flock of pigeons, all in different stages of lifting off into the air, each one a frozen poem.

Merit says she likes photography because photographs are a slice of the world. They focus on one small thing and eliminate everything else. I suppose that's why my photographs aren't as beautiful as hers—I want to gobble up the whole world in one entire gulp! BURP!

January 28, 1929

Dear Friend,

Eva snuck a bottle of her mother's fingernail polish today and painted our fingernails. WHEESH, does that stuff stink! It made my head all spinny and ringy. But when she was done—nails as red as berries! We waited for it to dry, then chipped it all *off, of course. Miss O'Conner says eleven-year-olds shouldn't wear nail polish!*

February 2, 1929

Dear Friend,

Today Eva stepped on a sharp horseshoe nail in Bryant Park that was buried in the snow—likely one that popped off some buggy horse parked there. Merit and I picked her up—each of Eva's arms slung over our shoulders, Merit and I each gripping an ankle—and we carried her all the way to her home in the Rogers Peet department store kitty-corner from the library. It was rush hour, so the sidewalks were crowded and icy. I made LOUD ambulance noises to get folks to move out of the way. I just hope Eva doesn't get an infection. Doctors—sheesh!

Viviani's heart warmed as she reread these memories, but the entries that she'd starred, she realized, were more a record of their experiences. They were examples of friendship, sure, but they didn't explain what friendship *was*. They weren't yet the kind of story that would stir your soul.

Viviani chewed on her pen as she thought about how to make the entry on their makeshift ambulance work. She chewed and thought, thought and chewed . . .

Ugh. Did all writers struggle this much? Did all writers wrestle with the best way to capture a feeling that passes like a heartbeat, or a thing as slippery and lovely as friendship? Did they struggle with how to describe the purply sheen of a pigeon, or the shadowy wet sensation of walking through fog, or the murky smells hanging in the city during summer—a combination of frying things and river ports and garbage? Choosing the tip-toppest word, selecting liquidy-loveable language? The toil!

Viviani thought surely she was the only one in the world who struggled *this much* with how to write.

"Firecracker?" Papa rapped on the door and pushed it open.

Viviani sat up, smiled. "Hi, Papa!"

He burst into laughter.

"What is it?"

Papa motioned to his face. "You've gone and grown a mustache, Viviani! Since when did you become such a strapping young fella?"

Viviani touched her face. Ink! *Everywhere.* She must have absentmindedly marked her face while writing.

Papa sat on the bed next to her. He smelled like his

workshop in the basement: a swirl of wood shavings, oil, and coal dust. He pulled a handkerchief from his cover-all pocket.

"Lick," he told her, and she licked a corner of the handkerchief. He began scrubbing her cheek.

"What'd you do today, Papa?"

"Today? Let's see. Today I was a telephone repairman and a furniture fixer and a pulley oiler and a tile spackler."

"And now you're a Viviani cleaner." Viv smiled.

Papa smiled, too. "And now I'm a Viviani cleaner. The best of the jobs. You ready for dinner?"

"I suppose." Viviani sighed. She somehow couldn't tell him about the prize involved with this latest homework assignment. But then again, stories kindled in Papa's soul. Maybe he could help. "Papa, how would you describe friendship?"

"Well now, I think that's downright impossible to do, don't you? Each friendship is as unique as the two people in it! After all, 'the language of Friendship is not words, but meanings.' Thoreau said that."

He mussed her hair before turning to leave. "Come down soon! Liverwurst tonight!"

Well, nuts.

If a writer as smart and famous as Henry David Thoreau couldn't describe friendship, how in the world was she supposed to?

Viviani picked at a scab on her knee. A tiny bead of blood appeared. She could hear the sounds of her family sitting around the table for dinner down the hall, but she didn't think she could eat a bite.

Maybe winning the contest wouldn't be as easy as she'd thought. And what kind of story collector would that make her?

CHAPTER FIVE

Fairy Tales,

Dewey Decimal 398.22

SEE ALSO: *Armenians—folklore; fairy poetry*

"I know exactly what story I'm going to write for the essay contest," Eva declared the following afternoon as they walked toward the library.

"You do?" Merit said.

Eva nodded. "It's based on an Armenian fairy tale. Want to hear it?"

"Absolutely," Viviani said quickly. She was surprised at the pang of jealousy she felt. But maybe listening to Eva's story would inspire Viviani to find hers.

"Okay." Eva took a deep breath and giggled. She was unused to having center stage. "Once there was a hen-house filled with the fattest, loudest, featheriest chickens that ever lived."

"Featheriest?" Merit asked, eyebrow raised.

Viviani elbowed her. Such a stickler, Merit could be! "Go on, Eva."

"These hens clucked and cooed and laid all sorts of beautiful, warm eggs. Brown eggs, spotted eggs—the hens were cozy and happy.

"One day, a wolf heard them gossiping, and he snuck inside the henhouse. *'Ha ha!'* he said, teeth flashing. 'Now you will be my lunch.'

"The hens flustered and clucked, but the eldest hen puffed out her wide breast. 'If you say so,' she said. 'But first won't you please sing us a song? I understand your voice is quite lovely, and I'd regret it ever so much if I died having never heard you sing.'"

The traffic light changed, and the girls skipped across Fifth Avenue. Eva continued, breathless. "A grin crept across the wolf's wide mouth. 'A song?' he said with pride. 'Well, I suppose a farewell song couldn't hurt.' And so he sang: a deep, bellowing howl from his heart."

Eva stopped at the base of the library stairs. Up on the terrace, volunteers from the American Library Association rang large handbells as they collected used books for troops overseas. "This is not a library return box!" one of them sang cheerily. "Books for troops!"

Eva shouted over the clanging: "The wolf howled his very best songs. The mama hen's best friend, the yard dog, heard him yowling and carrying on. The dog

43

dashed into the henhouse and chased the wolf away, taking a sizable bite out of his hindquarters."

Eva snapped her teeth with a ferocious, un-Eva-like growl, then blinked, like she'd surprised herself by telling that whole tale from memory. "The end."

Viviani and Merit laughed and applauded wildly (Viviani even whistled a little), and Eva curtsied. But as Viviani beamed at Eva, she felt a tiny twist of doubt. Eva's story was good. Could hers be that good, too? Good enough for the *Times*?

"What about you two?" Eva asked.

"I'm, er, not quite ready to share yet," Viviani blurted.

"Well, I can't wait to hear yours! How could your story not be amazing? You live in a *library*." Merit grinned. Viviani shrunk a bit, but Merit didn't seem to notice and continued, "I don't know what my story is going to be, exactly, but I know it'll be inspired by one of two photographs. Want to see them?"

"Yeah!" Viviani said a bit too loudly while Eva nodded. They followed Merit once again to the picture collection on the first floor. Mrs. Coe greeted them. Viviani thought she might live there, behind that desk. She dressed a bit old-timey, with high-neck blouses and long, full skirts. She looked like she hadn't moved from her spot in decades. Viviani had never *not* seen her there. She wondered if Mrs. Coe ever used the restroom. Or if she even ate.

Merit pulled a photograph from the Animals category. It showed a small short-haired dog and a big black-and-white cat—the duo were almost the same size—sharing a snack they'd obviously stolen from a picnic. A dirty plate lay in the grass nearby.

"Those sneaks!" Viviani said with a laugh.

Merit grinned and nodded. "You can see they've helped each other nab the food! The picture tells the whole story in a single image."

The trio of girls looked at the photo a moment longer. "Or . . . ," Merit said. She reshelved the cat-and-dog photo and pulled another photograph from the collection, this one a few rows over, from the People category.

"This one."

This photo was captioned "A Sympathetic Friend" and showed two women, both sitting, both wearing old-timey dresses, a lot like the clothes Mrs. Coe wore. One woman wore a white flower in her hair and was clasping the wrist of her friend. The friend held something—a letter?—and she touched her own face gently, as one does when truly sad, or truly deep in thought.

"Wow," breathed Eva. "What do you think is in that letter?"

"It's from the army," Viviani imagined straightaway. "Her husband died in the war."

Merit sighed. "Or it's a recipe written by her

45

grandmother, and this woman is remembering her *tayta* and her delicious *mahlab* bread."

Eva's fingers hovered lightly over the photo. Mrs. Coe cleared her throat, and Eva pulled her hand back. "Whatever it is, it's very important. The letter is the center of the photo. The focal point."

Merit smiled, and Viviani could see she was pleased that some of her photography lessons were sinking in.

Viviani tapped the table. "This one, Merit. You have to write about these women."

Merit looked at the image wistfully. "I think you're right."

Viviani sighed.

It is possible, Dear Friend, to feel pride and jealousy simultaneously. Viviani knew that for certain at this moment.

After eating a quick snack in the Fedeler apartment, Merit and Eva headed home. Viviani tapped a fork against her teeth, and Mama winced, turning up the radio: "Squeeze Me" by Fats Waller blasted through the jazzy airwaves.

"Mama," Viviani said, "I have to write a story for school about friendship, and I'm drawing a blank." For some reason, Viviani didn't tell her mother about the prize. Not yet. It felt like too much pressure, like a too-tight hug squeezing her ribs. She would mention it later, after she had a winning idea.

"Oh, surely not my little story collector? Storyless? Never!" Mama planted a firm kiss on the top of Viviani's red head.

Viviani knew it was meant to make her feel better. But her mother's words actually felt just like picking at that scab on her knee. Her parents were proud of her for being something she obviously was not. How could she let them down? She *had* to find a story.

"Well, where should I go for inspiration?"

Mama crossed one arm over her stomach, balanced her other elbow atop it, and rested her chin on her knuckles. "Gosh, Viviani. If I weren't so busy *living in a library*, with all those *librarians* available to *assist me*, I might be able to help you answer that question." She winked.

Viviani laughed and saluted Mama with two fingers. Mama could make her laugh even when she felt blue.

"Thanks, Mama! You're the darb!" And off Viviani dashed to find her story.

CHAPTER SIX

Curiosities and Wonders,

Dewey Decimal 032.02

SEE ALSO: *questions and answers, eccentrics and eccentricities*

Have you ever experienced a storytelling emergency? It feels rather like searching for a word that's *juuuust* on the tip of your tongue—you know the one: that valuable word that goes missing the moment you need it. That, Dear Friend, is how Viviani felt, seeking her story: like the idea was *right there*, waiting for Viviani to trip over it, capture it, bring it home, tame it, and call it her own. Her story was simply lost, hiding, and she would find it.

Viviani dashed up the stairs to the third floor and down the long, wide hallway. *Clap clap clap* went her shoes on the marble. "Slow down, Viviani!" yelled the day guard, Mr. Leon. But she couldn't slow down—this was, after all, a storytelling emergency!

She ran into the catalog room, through the grand double wooden doors, and into the Main Reading Room.

Viviani had been in this room almost every day of her life, and still, *still*, walking into it stole her breath away. Viviani's favorite part of the room was the ceiling: from it hung dozens of bronze chandeliers, each with long arms like an octopus's tentacles, holding massive globes of light. Behind the chandeliers hung a series of plaster carvings, curling and swirling and blooming like a well-tended mahogany garden. The carvings framed painted murals featuring blue skies and sunshine-rimmed clouds. They looked like windows to heaven.

The circulation desk in the Main Reading Room was a large, buttery-colored wooden beast, and three librarians buzzed around behind it. One of them took the book requests that library patrons had written on small scraps of paper, loaded them into metal canisters, and—*whoosh!*—sent them flying off in the vacuum of the pneumatic tubes mounted to the wall behind the desk. Viviani knew the canisters sank through the tubes and into the seven-story bookshelves just below this room. There, other librarians would pull the requested books from the miles-long stacks, then whisk them back up to the reading room in a dumbwaiter.

Whoosh! went another patron's book request. If she wrote down a wish for a story and sent it through those tubes, Viviani wondered, would her essay magically come squeaking up in the dumbwaiter?

"Hey," Viviani said to the remaining two librarians, Mr. Wilburforce and Miss Hoolihan. "I need inspiration for a homework assignment. Got any good friendship stories?"

"You'll have to be a bit more specific." Mr. Wilburforce smiled. "We're surrounded by twenty-two thousand books in this room alone!"

"You know what I mean." Viviani grinned.

Miss Hoolihan's lips thinned. "Viviani, you'll have to excuse us. We're in the middle of a crisis here."

"Crisis?" Viviani's ears perked. The best friendship stories began with a crisis! After all, the Moppets had originally teamed up to track down a missing stamp collection.

Mr. Wilburforce chuckled. "Now, hold on. I wouldn't exactly call this a crisis."

Miss Hoolihan fanned a stack of due-date cards. "Look here. Five—no, *six*—books, all of them rare medical volumes. Valuable books, these ones. *Real* valuable. All checked out on different dates, but all within days of each other. All overdue, all to the same address."

Viviani stood on tiptoe to see behind the counter. "And?"

Miss Hoolihan scowled. Honestly, one would think some of the librarians were fed a diet of lemons and sauerkraut. She spoke through flattened lips. "The name on each account is different."

Viviani still didn't understand. "And, *and*? Couldn't it just be an apartment building with a bunch of, I don't know, medical students living there or something?"

"Just what I was wondering," Mr. Wilburforce chimed in.

"Ah, but!" Miss Hoolihan said. She dug a stack of letters from a file folder. "I was just about to get to *this*. All the overdue letters we sent to that address? All came back to us this week, all marked as 'Return to Sender.' All of them say, 'No one here by that name.'"

"Okay," Viviani said. "Getting weirder." She tried to peer at the letters, but Miss Hoolihan swept them away.

"I'm going to this address tonight," Miss Hoolihan said, obviously pleased with her sleuthing skills. "I'm getting to the bottom of this."

Mr. Wilburforce smiled. "They'll turn up, I'm sure of it. Overdue books are an inconvenience to everyone, but I'd not say we're in crisis." Viviani agreed but couldn't resist the familiar tingle of a good story. Could this work as her essay? She appreciated a good mystery. She and Merit and Eva were amateur detectives, after all. They'd caught a criminal in the library just two short months ago. Boy, had that been exciting!

Viviani plopped down at a table right there and scribbled out an opening:

Once upon a time there were missing Once Upon a Times,
and it fell to the story collector to find them.

But when Viviani lifted her pen to write the next sentence, nothing came out. She was stumped. Sighing, she scratched through it. Nah, that wouldn't work. It made for a good mystery, but it wasn't about friendship.

"Keep me posted, Miss Hoolihan," Viviani said, looking up to where she and Mr. Wilburforce were still chatting. "And let me know if you need my help. I'm pretty good at mysteries, you know."

CHAPTER SEVEN

Tall Tales,

Dewey Decimal 398.2

SEE ALSO: *folklore, legendary characters*

At dinner that night (stewed beets—*blech!*), Edouard told the family all about the lecture he'd snuck into in the library auditorium that afternoon:

"It was about codes and codebreaking! The library has so many books on it!" The thought of using the books and resources at his very fingertips to encrypt codes had him all flustered. "Did you know that Leonardo da Vinci could *write backward*? You had to use a mirror to read it. And many folks think Shakespeare put codes in his plays. And Sir Arthur Conan Doyle wrote a whole story called 'The Adventure of the Dancing Men,' where Sherlock Holmes solves the murder because of a coded clue: each letter of the alphabet was represented by a dancing stick figure!"

Edouard's eyes grew wider and wider as he talked, spearing beets on his fork with gusto. "They discussed everything from the Phaistos Disc to Morse code," he continued, waving his beet-laden fork in the air. "I'm going to encrypt my next homework assignment!"

"Not sure your teachers would love that, Edouard," Mama said with a chuckle.

"Speaking of homework," Viviani mumbled around a mouthful of peas. Mama frowned. "I still need an idea. Mine all seem to have gone missing."

"For what?" Papa said.

"I need inspiration for an essay at school. I'm writing a story about friendship." Viviani quickly scooped more peas into her mouth so she didn't have to mention the prize. It simply felt *too big* if she talked about it.

Papa's face lit up. "Well, why didn't you say so?" Viviani grinned. She had come to the right place for a story.

After dinner, Papa got a hot cup of coffee and settled into his great stuffed armchair. The worn green chair was too small for Papa's large, lanky frame, but it was his favorite nonetheless. "You need a story, Viviani? Pull up a cushion, kids."

The three Fedelers scrambled to gather on the floor around Papa's chair. Mama stretched out on the couch. Story time with Papa was like watching stars glitter, like smelling roses in bloom, like splashing through the cool fountain in Bryant Park on a hot summer day. (Not that Viviani would know *anything* about that, Dear Friend. Ahem.)

"Friendship, eh?" Papa said, rubbing the stubble on his chin.

"You're friends with Thomas Edison, Papa," Edouard said. "Let's hear about him."

"Bor-*ing*," sang Viviani. "This story needs *action*. Not tinkering with inventions that don't usually work."

Papa laughed. "Action, eh? Okay, I have just the story for you. This one's about my buddy Edwin Burke, who I met in the navy."

"Yes!" John Jr. said, shifting on the floor. "I love a good raunchy sailor story."

"John Jr.," Mama said levelly.

He shrugged. "What? I do."

Viviani threw a pillow at him.

"So the *Minnesota*, that was my ship, you know. It docked in Washington. And there was this saloon there. A real dive, this place. Roaches, terrible food, watery drinks—the whole bit. It was perfect. Anyway, they were offering one hundred dollars to any man who could stand in a boxing ring for four minutes against some prizefighter."

"One hundred dollars!" Edouard said. He hugged his knees.

"Who was the boxer, Papa?" John Jr. said. "Say it was Jack Dempsey."

"Well now, that I don't recall. And here's why: no sooner had I ducked under those boxing-ring ropes than that boxer knocked me flat on my back. Out cold, I was. Huge cut over my eye, too. They dragged me out of the ring and threw a bucket of cold water in my face. I sputtered awake. Whole thing lasted maybe sixty seconds, from the ding of the bell to my ice-water bath."

At this point, Edouard and John Jr. jumped up and began acting out the story, Edouard taking a mock swing and socking John Jr.'s jaw. John spun and windmilled his arms in slow motion, taking long, heaving, exaggerated minutes to collapse in a heap. Edouard leapt about, arms overhead in a victory stance.

"What happened next, Papa? What about your buddy Edwin?" Viviani asked eagerly. Maybe this could work for her essay after all!

"He held out."

"He won the hundred dollars?" Edouard stopped leaping and returned to Papa's story in Washington.

"'Aye, there's the rub,'" Papa said, throwing in a little Shakespeare for good measure. "That rat of an owner only paid him fifty dollars."

Papa laughed, remembering it now. Edouard and John Jr. continued to box. But Viviani felt as impatient as a ticking clock. Her essay was due in a week! "What does that have to do with friendship?"

"Well, Firecracker, he used that fifty dollars to pay for my stitches!" Papa pointed to his brow—was that a faint scar, or was it really a wrinkle? He took a long swig of hot coffee. "Ah, now *that's* a good memory."

A good memory *and* a good story. One with value. Worth. Because it made everyone here smile. Would Viviani *ever* be able to tell a tale like that? This story wasn't *her* story; she couldn't use it. Plus, well, the thought of turning in a story with blood and stitches made her woozy.

Tick tick tick. Impatience swelled inside Viviani as she sat back, deep in thought. The essay was due in seven short days, and she still didn't even have an idea! All the stories she'd heard were about friends, but they didn't capture what friendship *meant*. Viviani knew in her heart if she could capture *that*—the feeling of finding a person whose soul smiles at yours—she'd win the contest for sure.

Boy, did she wish she were like Merit or Eva—*POOF!* Idea. *POOF!* Written. They made it look easy. It left her a little grumbly, honestly.

Tick tick tick.

CHAPTER EIGHT

Natural Disasters,
Dewey Decimal 904

SEE ALSO: *catastrophes, extreme weather*

*T*ick tick tick.

Six days.

Missing books from the library.

Unfound stories by the girl who lived there.

It seemed to Viviani there were lots of lost words wandering around out there in need of capture.

Something about those long-overdue books nibbled at Viviani's imagination. They were all medical journals, plus they were checked out under different names to the same address? There was definitely a pattern. Edouard *had* been reciting gobs of facts about codes . . .

Viviani's head snapped up. Could there be a hidden message in those medical titles?

She paced the length of the library, racking her brain. Codes in book titles? Normally, she would have loved the thought of uncovering secret meanings, but she didn't have time for any distractions. It took *ages* to crack a code. She needed a *story idea*, now. The fact that she hadn't yet had a single good idea weighed on her like a—well . . . *drat*. She couldn't even come up with a good, weighty simile!

Viviani groaned and flung her arms up, staring at the ceiling in frustration. The *ceiling*. She knew where she should go: the roof. From there see could see hundreds of people, a story illuminating each one of them like a moonbeam. She'd find inspiration up there for sure.

She climbed several sets of stairs, hurled open the heavy metal door to outside marked EMPLOYEES ONLY, and stepped into the bright sunlight.

The pigeons John Jr. had captured clucked in their cages. Viviani scooped a handful of feed and tossed it to them. They pecked at one another, battling for the seeds. "You guys aren't very good at being friends," she said to the flock.

John Jr. was up there, too, looking through a huge pair of black binoculars, then marking something in pencil on a notepad. He lifted the binoculars to his eyes again.

"Please tell me you aren't spying on people," Viviani said, sliding beside him.

"I'm not spying on people." He lowered his binoculars and scrawled in the notepad: *3:43 p.m. Corner of 42nd and 5th.*

"What *are* you doing?"

"I'm noting the times of the trolley stops," John Jr. said. He didn't lower the binoculars but waved in the general direction of the trolley clanging along four stories below, down on Fortieth Street. "Carroll and I think if we can nail the timing of it perfectly, the driver won't notice when we hop on the back, and we can ride for free."

3:45 p.m. Corner of 42nd and 4th.

Viviani shook her head. "That's not going to work." She paused, chin in hand, looking down on Manhattan. "I'm still looking for inspiration for my essay."

"Well, why didn't you say so?" John Jr. dropped the binoculars, letting them sway around his neck. "I got a million stories!"

"I don't know, John." Viviani grinned. John's stories tended to be about pirates and cowboys and mischief and mayhem. "It needs to be about friendship."

"Friendship! Well, let me remind you of what happened to me and my old buddy Bobby Hoffman."

"Oh, I'm not sure about that."

"Remember, Bobby lived in the Mechanics and Tradesmen's Institute next to that big Tennis and Racquet Club . . ."

"Yeah, but—"

"And remember, the day this story takes place, it'd dumped a ton of snow—like eight inches. This was . . . last year. Anyways, we climbed up to *his* rooftop and made a huge, three-foot-around snowball."

Viviani sighed. John Jr. was on a roll now. There would be no interrupting him. "I remember."

"Anyways, we got the bright idea to push that monster snowball from the roof. We thought it would drop right off the edge of the institute and into the alley, but *hooboy!* Were we wrong!"

"Yep."

"That snowball arced perfectly onto the roof of the racquet club next door. It was like watching it happen underwater, Viv. It went right through a skylight—crash! And boom, boom, boom, all the way down into the kitchen, ten whole floors below. Lucky that no one was killed."

John Jr. shook his head, grinning sheepishly. "Never seen Papa so mad."

"Neither have I." Viviani giggled. Yep. Mischief and mayhem.

They both paused, and the city buzzed beneath them. "So," Viviani said, "what does that have to do with friendship?"

"Viv, when you get in that much trouble with a friend, *nothing* brings you closer together."

Viviani laughed and shook her head. "Adults like Miss Hutch won't give a prize to a story about breaking the rules."

John Jr. perked. "There's a prize?"

Viviani blinked and shrugged off the question. "Sort of."

She was starting to feel guilty about not telling her family about the *Times*, but expectations can feel itchy-tight, like a shrunken wool sweater. "Thanks anyways, but I think I need to look for inspiration elsewhere."

John Jr. resumed timing the trolleys. "Suit yourself. It's still a great story."

Viviani thought of other great stories, like her favorite books: *Five Children and It*. The Camp Fire Girls series. *The Wouldbegoods*. They were all tales of adventure, featuring interesting kids who always managed to flub things up. They were naughty and funny and risk-takers, the siblings in those stories. Like John Jr. and his mischief and mayhem. She decided to try her hand at a story like that.

Leaving John to his binoculars, she found a quiet corner of the library, cracked open her captain's log, and began:

TANK YOU VERY MUCH

by Viviani Fedeler

There once was a family named Tank who fancied themselves the best pranksters in all the land. There was Tink Tank who excelled at sleight-of-hand card tricks. Then came Tonk Tank who could build traps and snares like no one else. Finally, there was Bitty Tank the littlest Tank of them all, but oh, was she the one to watch out for!

Was it the beginning of a fun story? Yes, Viviani thought so. Was it about friendship? No. Viviani groaned and snapped her captain's log shut. She'd finish this tale later, just to see where it went. (Her characters often surprised her with their antics!) But she'd have to keep seeking to find her missing tale of friendship.

She needed a story worth telling. But what did that even *mean*?

Viviani wandered the stairwells, pondering that question, when she found Edouard in the small radio booth inside the library, chatting with the WJZ announcer.

"Fact," Edouard was saying. "Radio receivers use a very fine wire called a cat's whisker to find the radio signal."

"You don't say." The announcer leaned back in his chair, nodding.

"*Pssst!* Edouard!" Viviani loud-whispered. She never

knew when the large metal microphone was on ("hot," as Edouard would say), so she was overly cautious around it. "I need your help."

Edouard shot a suspicious look over his horn-rimmed glasses. "With what?"

"I still need a story."

Edouard beamed. *This* was his specialty. This was *every* Fedeler's specialty, it seemed. Every Fedeler but Viviani. "Fiction or nonfiction?"

"I guess . . . it doesn't matter?"

Edouard hopped out of his chair and started up the stairs. He scoffed. "It always matters, Viv. Meticulously researched nonfiction is the purest form of storytelling. Come on."

Normally, Viviani would roll her eyes, but now she wondered if a story like this might indeed be a good way to go. After all, the *New York Times* was nonfiction. Perhaps she could write a true story about, say, Billy the Pygmy Hippo, President Coolidge's pet hippopotamus, which lived at the National Zoo. With his animal friends. That might be worthy of an award!

Edouard and Viv wound their way back up to the Main Reading Room (*sigh!*), past Mr. Wilburforce behind the large central desk, and toward the pink marble doorframe at the south end of the building. The Rare Books Room.

Viviani didn't visit this room often, because it was

small and locked and, well—it was a dead end. If, say, you went in there while playing hide-and-seek with your brothers, you couldn't get back out without getting tagged. (*Ahem.* Yes, Friend, she knew this from experience.)

The books behind these leather-wrapped doors were so valuable that the door was kept locked at all times. A lot of these books could not even be loaned or checked out. Edouard stepped up to the door and rapped sharply. Moments later, the door swung open. Miss Fillipelli, the librarian in charge of this collection, beamed when she saw Edouard (as all the librarians did; Edouard was their mascot of sorts, their gold standard for reading and curiosity).

"Come in, come in," Miss Fillipelli said, standing aside. The musty smell of old books washed over Viviani, and she felt as though she were floating atop the scent.

The Rare Books Room showcased many books sporting thick leather covers with gold-embossed titles. The pages of the books were yellowed, their spines crumbling. Most of the titles weren't in English or were in a version of English that Viviani found impossible to decipher.

"Are you here to see *Cunningham's Text-book of Anatomy* again, Mr. Fedeler?"

Viviani rolled her eyes—*Mr. Fedeler!*

Edouard bowed deeply, like a knight addressing a princess. "If you please, madam."

Miss Fillipelli giggled and shuffled away. She took her job as guardian of rare tomes very seriously—she wore no makeup, no jewelry, no perfume, and kept her fingernails trimmed tight. She wore nothing that could harm these texts in any way.

Miss Fillipelli returned with *Cunningham's Text-book of Anatomy*. It was a crumbling old medical book, with yellowed pages and a soft, worn cover. The aged leather and pages felt soft to Viviani's touch.

Edouard opened the book gently and flipped through the tissue-thin pages. "I found this after seeing all those books in Dr. Monroe's office. Look!"

The book was gorgeously, thoroughly illustrated: one picture showed all the stringy red muscles beneath skin, another depicted the red and blue veins tunneling through the body, like roads and rivers on a map. And one picture featured a complete skeleton, bones linked, drawn from several different angles.

"Did I hear someone mention Dr. Monroe?" a voice called out. "I don't usually do house calls, but for you Fedelers . . . well, your house is special."

Viviani and Edouard spun and were greeted by a set of tired, friendly eyes peering through a pair of bottle-thick glasses.

"Benjamin!" Viviani said, smiling at the doctor's apprentice.

Benjamin smiled back. "Yes, and you are . . . Edouard, is it?" They both chuckled.

"Are you studying?" Viviani asked.

"Always. Between my job and my classes and, well— I'm always looking at a book. Which one are you looking at now?"

The trio turned back to the book, which was still open to the illustration of a skeleton. Edouard said, "*Cunningham's Text-book of Anatomy.*"

Benjamin adjusted his glasses. "Yes, a beautiful book. I've studied it several times."

Viviani ran her fingers lightly over the skull, the rib cage. She'd seen skeletons before, of course—Dr. Monroe even had a creepy skull sitting on one of her bookshelves. But seeing all the pieces assembled, like an intricate jig-saw puzzle, always fascinated Viviani.

"Wow," she breathed. "Hard to imagine this is inside every one of us."

"Fact," Edouard whispered. "All adult humans have two hundred and six bones."

Benjamin nodded. "We're all exactly alike, at our core."

They looked at the skeleton a moment longer until Benjamin cleared his throat. "Excuse me," he said, motioning to a table piled high with books. "I must get back to my work." He disappeared behind a stack.

"No wonder he always looks so tired," Viviani whispered to Edouard. "All work and no play." She tapped the skeleton on the page. "I'm going to name her Miss Bones. Can you imagine what she'd look like dancing?"

Edouard smiled. "Clackety, I guess. Lots of chattering teeth and clicking joints. Miss Bones. I like that."

Viviani sighed. "She's wonderful. I'm just not sure she's the muse for my winning story."

"Unless she befriends Mr. Muscles and Queen Veins from a few pages back," Edouard suggested.

Viviani shuddered. Writing a story with all this medical stuff? It immediately brought to mind those gleaming needles and scalpels in Dr. Monroe's office.

Doesn't one have to *love* what they write? She wasn't sure this was the route. They scooted out of the Rare Books Room.

"But I *need* that book!" someone was saying to Mr. Wilburforce as Viviani and Edouard passed the circulation desk in the Main Reading Room. "I'm going to miss my deadline without that information."

Deadline? Viviani listened carefully. Surely this was a writer!

The woman who stood opposite Mr. Wilburforce wore a tight jaw, tight haircut, and tight pants. *Pants!*

Sure, Viviani had seen women in pants around the city, but this woman wore *pants* to the *library*! So bold!

"I'm sorry, ma'am, but I told you: that title is checked out. Overdue, unfortunately. But checked out."

The woman ran her hand through her hair so roughly that Viviani thought strands of it might come out. "Any chance you'd tell me who . . ."

"No. I cannot tell you who has that book, Miss Hickok."

Miss Hickok nodded furiously, as though she understood but didn't like the answer. She ran her hands through her hair again. "Okay, okay. Just—call me the *minute* that book is returned, okay? Lorena Hickok. The *New York Times*." She tapped a piece of paper on the desk, slid it toward Mr. Wilburforce. It apparently had that exact information scrawled on it.

The New York Times?! Viviani's heart cartwheeled. But before Viviani could introduce herself as a fellow writer, the reporter turned on her heel and rushed out the door, muttering a gruff "excuse me" as she pushed past Viviani and Edouard.

"She's intense," someone said over Viviani's shoulder. She jumped and turned to find that Benjamin had walked up behind them.

Edouard shrugged. "She can't find the book she needs. I'd be intense, too."

"That's true," Benjamin said. "There's nothing more

frustrating than not being able to find the right information." He nodded resolutely and left the Main Reading Room as well.

Viviani rushed toward the desk. "Mr. Wilburforce—was that woman with the *New York Times*?"

Mr. Wilburforce frowned. "You know I can't tell you that, Viviani. She's a library patron."

"So I guess you can't tell me which book she's requesting, either?" Maybe *this* could be how Viviani would find her winning story. It wouldn't really be cheating . . . would it? Not cheating—*sleuthing*. Viviani was just using her sleuthing skills to find out what kind of stories interested this reporter. Right?

Mr. Wilburforce didn't even bother answering, just scowled more deeply.

"Okay, okay," Viviani said. She knew the rules. No one outside of library staff was allowed to know who was reading what. Violation of privacy and whatnot. Those kinds of rules were put in place during the Great War, when all sorts of important folks used the library for top secret research. There were rumors of spies sneaking into the library to craft codes and study rare maps. Viviani often imagined them tiptoeing about, tapping out Morse code with their pencil points, or writing messages on book margins in invisible ink. John Jr. had told her the study rooms on the second floor were where they met to exchange secrets.

Were there spies *here*, *now*? Viviani scanned the faces of the strangers studying at the rows and rows of tables around her. She was yanked back to the moment by a loud gasp.

Mr. Wilburforce snatched the piece of paper on which Miss Hickok had scrawled her book request.

"What is it?" Edouard asked. Viviani was grateful to him for that; the librarians *adored* Edouard.

"Well, I'm not telling you anything here, but . . ." Mr. Wilburforce leaned toward the Fedeler kids and looked left and right, as though he really *were* sharing something a bit secretive.

"I just realized that the book Miss Hickok is requesting? It's one of the missing titles Miss Hoolihan is trying to track down."

Viviani felt a grin grow. If multiple people were all seeking the same missing rare books, there was *definitely* a pattern here. Books that rare only get checked out once every few years, if that. To have them sought out so frequently? There was definitely a code to crack. This had the familiar whiff of a good mystery! Perhaps if she and the Moppets could find these overdue books before her friendship essay was due in six days, *that* could be her winning story. Plus, she'd be helping a reporter for the *New York Times*!

This plan had to work. Had to!

CHAPTER NINE

Storytelling,

Dewey Decimal 372.6

SEE ALSO: *folklore, literature*

*T*ick tick tick.

Five days! Five days to write and turn in her essay, which meant five days to solve the mystery of the overdue books. If she couldn't figure out where the missing books had gone, her chances of winning the contest plummeted. Because solving this pattern was an award-winning idea; of this, Viviani was certain. This story had everything a great story needed: Mystery! Intrigue! Books! Possibly spies! And surely there was a friendship angle in there, too? But oh, *five days*! It couldn't be done, could it?

Well, she'd have to keep looking for other story ideas, too, of course. *Just in case.* Papa always said, *"Just in case* saves me more often than the initial case!" Plus, it simply never hurt to collect more stories.

"Will you stop pacing, Viv?" Eva said, looking up from her illustration. Illustration! Eva had already finished her essay and had decided to add illustrations. Eva, Viviani, and Edouard were now working in the map room, just before the library closed for the day, just before Viv was set to meet Mr. Green.

Viviani paused her pacing. "Hey, why are you drawing upside down?" Eva was studying one of the photographs Mrs. Coe had helped her find, of chickens, foxes, and dogs, but she was looking at it topsy-turvy.

"You can capture something . . . *different* when you see what you're drawing as just a bunch of shapes and shadows," she said. "Sometimes it helps to turn things upside down to see them as they really are."

Edouard straightened his glasses. "Fact: the naturalist John Muir used to flip upside down to look at the world when he got stumped by a problem."

Viviani just so happened to be stumped by a problem! "You mean, a flip in the air?" Viviani asked excitedly. "Like an acrobat?"

"No, no." Edouard screeched his chair backward, stood, spread his feet wide, and bent at the waist. He looked through his legs at the wall of maps and globes that was, technically, behind him.

Viviani tried it immediately. Feet wide, bent at the waist—*allez-oop!* Upside down.

"Ugh. It's just making me dizzy."

Viviani continued to pace the red-tile floors of the now-empty map room. Eva had finished drawing, Edouard had finished calculating, and now it was just her. Her and her pacing.

She adored this room. The windows were large—two stories!—and let in so much sunlight that the golden carved ceiling sometimes looked aflame during the early-morning hours. But best of all, the room was stuffed with oversized, colorful maps and smooth, spinning globes. Maps of the universe. Maps of Central Park. And maps of everything in between.

The library had closed for the day, with the ornate iron doors locked shut—*BOOM!*—in front of the revolving entryway. For the next hour or so, the librarians and administrative staff would wander the halls, and then they, too, would leave. Then just a handful of folks—Viviani and her family; the custodian, Mr. Green; and Mr. Eames, the night guard—would be the only ones creeping around inside this massive marble building.

Viviani dug out a fifteenth-century map covered in illustrations of sea monsters. She recalled hearing a myth that one breed of sea monster was so large, it had trees and grass and flowers sprouting on its back. It would float in the high seas, anchored in the waves like an island. Wooden sailing ships would dock there, and *sploosh!* The sea monster would curl up on itself, dragging the lot of them down down down to the floor of the sea. The only thing left of the fleet were the bubbles floating to the surface—*ploop! plip! ploop!* The lush greenery on its back was bait. The sea monster had successfully fished for its supper!

Could *that* be her just-in-case friendship story? Maybe a heroic tale of sailors who banded together to defeat a monster?

Hmph. The mystery of the missing books and the friends who find them was better. Viviani walked to the window and knelt on the narrow ledge. The glass was cool against her forehead, her breath steaming the window. From here, she could see the back side of Leo Lenox, one of the marble lions perched in front of the library.

"Lenox, should you and Leo Astor over there be my just-in-case story?" She arched her neck to see the second lion, at the opposite corner of the library terrace. Perhaps a story about how the real Mr. Lenox and the real Mr. Astor both started libraries, and how they teamed up to make *this* library. Hey, that wasn't a half-bad idea. She'd heard dozens and dozens of tour guides tell the story over the years. She could tell it, but from

75

the lions' point of view. She grabbed her captain's log and began writing:

Leo Lenox loved books. Leo Astor loved books. Unfortunately, they loved books apart from each other.

Viviani shook her head, struck a line through *apart from each other*. That was a *terrible* way to start a story about friendship. Gosh, choosing the exact right phrase was so hard. She leaned her head against the cool glass again.

"Git yer head off of there, missy!" Mr. Green, the custodian, had snuck into the room. Viviani leapt. No one *ever* heard Mr. Green coming; he was like a cat. He'd win at Master Thief for sure. "Do you know how hard them windows are to clean?"

"Heavens, Mr. Green, why do you always sneak up like that?" Viviani laid her fingertips on her chest.

"I ain't sneaking. You just ain't listening. Always got yer head in the clouds."

"Aw, thank you, Mr. Green."

"I didn't mean it nice."

"I know." Viviani grinned and hopped off the window ledge. She moved to one of the big carved-oak tables. "Ready for our lesson?"

Viviani and Mr. Green had been meeting in the map room every week so she could help him improve his reading. She had thought about postponing this lesson to focus on the mystery, on her story, but she knew how much Mr. Green looked forward to their lessons. As did she.

Mr. Green tucked a greasy strand of blond hair behind his ear. "Ready." He reached into his satchel and pulled out—

"Again?" Viviani said with a sigh.

Mr. Green opened the orange, yellow, and black cover of *Millions of Cats*. "This book is great. That drawing of all them cats piled up together . . ." Mr. Green chuckled. If you had told Viviani Fedeler three months earlier that she'd sit beside Mr. Green and watch him chuckle over *Millions of Cats*, she would've said you were full of malarkey. Why, John Jr. had once told Viv that Mr. Green was a cannibal! She knew it wasn't true (well, after a while she did), but still.

Mr. Green flipped to page one and pointed a ragged fingernail at the first sentence. "Once upon a time there was a very old man and a very old . . . wo . . . woman."

"Perfect," Viviani said, beaming. He was getting very good at sounding out the words.

Mr. Green slowly read the story through to the refrain, which he practically sang: "Hundreds of cats, Thousands of cats, Millions and billions and trillions of cats."

Viviani suspected that Mr. Green wanted to read this

story so often because it was familiar and comfortable. Which was great when you were learning to read.

Was she doing the same thing, learning to write? Sticking to the familiar, rather than stretching and twisting and pulling her imagination as far as she could?

Viviani sighed and buried her head in her hands. She was. The story of Leo Astor and Leo Lenox wasn't *her* story. It didn't work as her friendship story, not even as a just-in-case. It simply wasn't what she wanted to say about something as complicated and important as *friends*! Why, thinking about Eva and Merit and their adventures together? Friendship was safe and familiar, sure, but it also *wasn't*. Friendship led to nighttime capers in haunted libraries. Friendship led to misunderstandings and occasionally (and unfortunately) lies. Friendship led to sometimes-painful total honesty. As majestic and dignified as Leo Astor and Leo Lenox were, a just-in-case story about them fell short of describing something as slippery and lovely as a friendship.

No, the mystery of the overdue books was the only story with promise, because it had all those elements: misunderstandings, probably lies, and likely painful honesty. She'd just have to focus on that for now, so she could not only find those books but also win that contest and prove herself a true story-collector-turned-storyteller.

Mr. Green reached the last page of *Millions of Cats* and grinned. "Want to start again?"

Viviani nodded. "Yes, I do. I want to start again."

Dear Friend,

The ONLY story that interests me is the mystery of the missing books. But I don't know how it ends! What kind of story has no ending? A story with no Happily Ever After is just words, wandering aimlessly, worrying their wordy hands, plodding their plotless feet.

What are those overdue titles trying to tell us? I know there's a pattern there, a code to crack. I need to ask Miss Hoolihan if I can get a gander at those due-date cards. There's a cipher in there, playing hide-and-seek with us, and I feel like I'm "It," searching for clues. Come on idea: olly, olly oxen free!

A just-in-case story is smart, I know. But that's not sparking anything, either. What do I do if there is no just-in-case? Is there such a thing as a just-in-case just-in-case?

Five days!

CHAPTER TEN

Investigation,
Dewey Decimal 363.289

SEE ALSO: *private investigators*

Have you noticed, Dear Friend, that when a person feels joy, it makes itself known through skipping and singing? Contentment, through solid, sure steps. Pensiveness results in meandering. But melancholy? Melancholy looks like the dragging of a thirty-pound anchor.

Viviani dragged her feet down the long length of the second-floor hallway. After being stumped on both story ideas and leads on missing books, no one had to tell her to stop skipping or to slow it down.

Being a story collector meant you always had the right words at the right time, like Papa. Being a story collector meant you knew exactly how someone else felt, like

Mama. Being a story collector meant you had big ideas and bigger plans, like John Jr. and Edouard.

Viviani wanted to be all those things. She felt that she was none of them. Merit, Eva . . . yes. Her . . . no.

She kicked the toes of her shoes as she walked. She knew she shouldn't—that sometimes left angry black scuffs on the marble that were terrible to buff out. But her spirits were so low, she could barely muster the oomph it took to put some pep in her step.

She'd better not let Mama see her like this. She'd be back at that doctor's office lickety-split.

"Four days," Viviani muttered. "I have four days to write something amazing. I have four days to find answers to mysteries. Can wonderful words appear in four short days?"

As she neared her apartment, the delicious smell of matzo ball soup floated toward her, yet it did little to lift her mood.

A handful of librarians—in Viviani's mind, she thought of a group of librarians as a *stack*—drifted out of the administrative offices. Miss Hoolihan was part of this stack.

Perhaps there was an update on the overdue books?

"Miss Hoolihan? Oh, Miss Hoolihan!" Viviani shouted, chasing after the stack. The librarians shushed her as one, *"Shhhhhhh!"* Viviani smiled. They did this even after hours. Habit.

"Miss Hoolihan, what's the latest on those overdue books?" Viviani asked. The librarian paused, but the others kept moving.

Miss Hoolihan looked over each shoulder and leaned in, as if sharing a conspiracy theory. "I went by that address—you know. The one given for all those different names?"

"Yeah?"

"Yes. And it was a deli! Owner told me no one lives there. He didn't know the first thing about the overdue books. Says he loves the library, but has never checked out those particular books."

"And you believe him?"

Miss Hoolihan nodded. "I think someone is holding on to those rare books. I came up here to try to find Mr. Bergquist. I think it's time to bring him in."

"Mr. Bergquist? Really?"

Miss Hoolihan bit her lip. "Yes, I think so."

"Wow," Viviani breathed. Mr. Bergquist was the library's special investigator. He was one of only six library investigators in the *whole country*. It was his job to track down missing books. And from what Viviani heard, he was very good at his job. And very busy. So busy, she'd never even met him, only seen him scurry urgently about the library. "Why Mr. Bergquist?"

"Those books, Viviani," Miss Hoolihan said, "they are

rare. And valuable. Worth over four thousand dollars. We really must find them. Mr. Bergquist wasn't in today, but I feel confident it's time for him to take a look at this."

Viviani's eyes widened. Four thousand dollars—wowza! Why, you could buy a home and all the furniture inside with that load of dough!

"Miss Hoolihan," Viviani said, chewing on her bottom lip, "can my friends and I go with you when you tell Mr. Bergquist about this case?"

"This *case* . . . ," Miss Hoolihan said, as if the taste of that word were overly salty. Chewy. Like old beef jerky. She apparently didn't like the sound of being involved in an investigation. She tugged on the hem of her cardigan.

"It's just that, well, my friends and I? The Moppets? We've solved a case before, you know. You may have seen an article written up about us a few months ago."

Miss Hoolihan didn't seem convinced.

"We just want to listen to the details as you share them with Mr. Bergquist. Please?" Viviani was desperate. This was her story—she just knew it. "I'll . . . I'll volunteer to reshelve books for you for a week!"

Miss Hoolihan laughed. "You don't have to do that, Viviani. I suppose just listening to the facts doesn't hurt."

Viviani bounced on her toes. "Thank you, Miss Hoolihan! You won't be sorry. With the Moppets on the case, we'll help you recover those overdue books."

Viviani skipped into the apartment, her melancholy anchor left behind.

Wow—another mystery! She couldn't wait to tell Eva and Merit. Viviani hoped the trio could crack open the case and her writer's block at the same time!

CHAPTER ELEVEN

Famous Detectives,
Dewey Decimal 364.152

SEE ALSO: *detectives—United States; detectives and mysteries*

The next day, Viviani, Merit, and Eva were popping and zinging like telegram wires as they waited in the second-floor office with Miss Hoolihan. At last, a petite woman wearing precise red lipstick and sporting perfect pin curls invited them inside.

"Hello, I'm Mr. Bergquist's assistant."

"Assistant! Ah, Watson, I presume," Viviani said, bowing. "And we await Sherlock."

The woman laughed. "Actually, I go by Miss Schneider. Can I get you anything while you wait? Water? Coffee?"

"I'd like a coffee, please," Miss Hoolihan said.

"Me, too," Viviani chimed in. Miss Schneider raised

an eyebrow but, sure enough, filled two steaming mugs. At last—a place where she'd be taken seriously!

Viviani added a touch of milk and six heaping spoonfuls of sugar before tasting it. "Blech! This coffee tastes like mud!"

Miss Schneider chuckled. "I think so, too. I prefer tea myself."

"Miss Schneider, what is it like to be a book detective?" Merit asked, jumping right in, Merit-style. She'd brought along her camera, and Viviani could tell her fingers were itching to take photographs of the crime scene.

"Well, we—" Miss Schneider began.

"Ooh!" Viviani said, placing her mug of mud on a desk beside her. "Do you have some of those spying tools? Like a recording device in your lipstick or . . ." Her eyes swept the room, landing on a framed photograph of a family. She crept closer and waved at it. "In here? Is there a camera in here? *Helloooooooooooo!*"

Eva shrank away nervously from the frame. Miss Hoolihan rolled her eyes and tugged on the edge of her cardigan. "Don't be silly, Viviani. There's no camera in there." But the librarian cleared her throat and flipped over the frame nonetheless.

"I bet you cut holes in newspapers and spy on bad guys," Merit added. "I saw them do that at the movies once. It looks like you're reading the paper, *la la la*, but

86

you're actually peeping at them through a little window in the newsprint."

"Well, we—" Miss Schneider began again.

"Do you carry around a big spyglass?" Eva interrupted. "Where are your trench coat and hat? Don't you all wear a trench coat and hat?"

At that moment, a large white-haired gentleman bumbled into the room. A stack of books was tucked under one arm, and he clutched a paper cup in his fist. He sloshed a refill of muddy coffee into his cup and swilled some of it.

"Morning, ladies," he said, shuffling around in his smallish office. He plopped down into a spinning desk chair and dropped the books onto a nearby pile. The nameplate on his desk read G. WILLIAM BERGQUIST.

"The book detective!" Eva whispered loudly. She blushed when she realized everyone heard her.

"As I was saying," Miss Schneider said at last, "we don't refer to ourselves as *book detectives*. The library actually calls us special investigators."

Merit flipped open a notebook and wrote that down. Viviani smiled to herself—notes! *Nice work, Merit.*

"Tell me what concerns you, Miss Hoolihan," he said to the librarian. He didn't look how Viviani imagined a detective would. He was large-framed, but both his voice and his eyes were gentle and kind. He looked like a friendly grandpa who gave great hugs, not a detective chasing bad guys down shady alleys.

Miss Hoolihan laid out her evidence while Merit took copious notes. The librarian showed Mr. Bergquist the check-out cards with long-overdue return dates. She explained that they were all valuable, rare medical books, all checked out within days of one another, all to the same address. "But they were checked out under different names. And the address turned out to be—"

"A deli!" Viviani interrupted. She was so excited, she felt like she would burst out of her skin. "Can you believe it?"

Mr. Bergquist removed his tiny wire-frame spectacles and peered at the check-out cards while chewing on the temple of his glasses. "That's unusual."

"What's unusual?" Merit asked, pencil at the ready.

"Well," he said, slipping his glasses back on, "we're not dealing with a thief, I'd say. Criminals don't usually bother with checking out a book."

"But there is something odd about all these rare medical volumes being overdue, right? Checked out to the same address?" Viviani asked.

Mr. Bergquist nodded, slurped more coffee. "Yes, it appears so. There is definitely a pattern here."

"A pattern!" Viviani exclaimed. So it *was* some sort of code. That's exactly what codes were—encrypted patterns!

Viviani chewed her bottom lip. "Can Merit take a photo of those check-out cards, Mr. Bergquist? We'd like to help analyze those titles. Look for the patterns you've mentioned."

Mr. Bergquist glanced at his assistant, and Miss Schneider smiled. "I don't see why not," she replied. "Take a photo, and we'll keep the originals here."

Viviani fanned them out on Mr. Bergquist's messy desk, and Merit took a quick photo. Miss Schneider scooped them up and placed them in a file folder.

Miss Hoolihan stood, tugging the hem of her cardigan so hard that Viviani was surprised it didn't unravel. It was obvious that she was both pleased that her hunch about the overdue books had been correct, and frustrated that these valuable books were now officially missing.

"How long will it take to locate these books, do you reckon?" Ms. Hoolihan asked. Viviani was grateful she did; Viviani had a deadline, after all. In three days.

Mr. Bergquist sighed. "Maybe three"—*yes!*—"years." *What? Oh no!*

"Three years!" Ms. Hoolihan cried, echoing Viviani's surprise. "With all due respect, sir, we must try and find those books as soon as possible."

Three years was quite a bit late to turn in her essay, Viviani thought glumly.

"Or more," Mr. Bergquist said.

Miss Hoolihan practically whimpered. "Mr. Bergquist, usually an overdue book is merely an inconvenience, like a splinter in your thumb. But these books are different. These books are so rare, they are the only place in the United States that contains *that exact* information. If we lose those books, we lose that medical knowledge. Gone. Lost forever. *That's* how rare they are. We will have patients out there suffering because that information is sitting on someone's bookshelf instead. These books are no splinter. These books are a support beam."

Viviani was, for once, speechless. Now she understood why Miss Hoolihan was so worked up. She'd never thought about what it meant for a book to be truly *rare*. To be the only record in the whole world of a specific piece of information? What a hefty responsibility those books had! They were beyond priceless.

Mr. Bergquist obviously felt that responsibility, too, based on how his jaw tightened. "Well, now that does change the stakes, doesn't it? Thank you for letting us know. And rest assured, we are specialists at what we do, Miss Hoolihan, just like you. We'll find those books as quickly as we can. Your medical students will be studying them again soon. I promise."

Miss Hoolihan wrung her hands but nodded. "Thank you, Mr. Bergquist. I appreciate you making this your highest priority. I don't think I'm exaggerating when I say that the health of New York City is depending on you. Perhaps the health of the entire United States." She gave the hem of her cardigan one last tug, then left.

Viviani and the Moppets quickly thanked Mr. Bergquist and Miss Schneider for their time and rushed into the hallway to make plans.

"Wow," Eva said. "We've got to find those books."

"We will," said Viviani. "Shake on it."

Merit, Eva, and Viviani performed their secret handshake, developed by Eva specially for three people: each girl linked a pointer finger with another girl's pinkie finger, each pinkie finger in turn linked with a pointer finger, all in a triangle.

Once linked, Viviani whispered, "Those books are rare. Rare and valuable, like old friends. Let's find those overdue books, Moppets."

And they shook on it: *one, two, three!*

CHAPTER TWELVE

Codes,

Dewey Decimal 652.8

SEE ALSO: *ciphers, signs and symbols*

"This is worrisome. Very, very worrisome."

Some statements, when expressed in just the right tone, can freeze time. With just a few words, Friend, you can be immobilized, your heart stopped, making you question your choices of late, just in case the statement refers to *you*.

So when Viviani heard those words—*This is worrisome*—she paused in her tracks and ran through everything she'd done this week, cataloging which *this* of *hers* someone might consider worrisome: the *this* when she jammed some of the typewriter keys in the administrative offices and couldn't get them unstuck? The *this* when she tried to cram Edouard's coat through the book return and couldn't get it unstuck? The *this* when she pushed all the elevator buttons at once and couldn't get the car unstuck?

(It seemed to Viviani now, upon such quick reflection, that she got a lot of things stuck.)

Today's *This is worrisome* was from Dr. Edwin Anderson, the library director, and indeed, worry swelled inside his every word.

He worked his jaw to and fro as Miss Hoolihan and Miss Schneider showed him the overdue check-out cards, explaining the vast value of the missing books. The staff were gathered in Astor Hall near the information desk, as they did every morning before the doors opened, to rally for the day. Viviani and Edouard happened to be walking through on their way to school, but Viviani immediately slowed. This she had to hear.

"Friends, this is our number one priority," he told the staff. "If your department has any suspiciously overdue books, please alert Miss Schneider at once. While overdue books are not a crime, we desperately need to find those that are currently misplaced. That information could literally save someone's life." Miss Hoolihan nodded emphatically.

Dr. Anderson continued. "Ralph Waldo Emerson said, 'Nature and books belong to the eyes that see them.' Our library books are meant to belong to all. This person—this *hoarder*—is robbing others of that opportunity. It is not the value of the books we seek to recover, friends. It is the value of the information they contain."

Viviani knew at that moment that she and the Moppets had to *find that story hoarder.*

"Tell me what you know about codes, Edouard," Viviani said. A blast of cold air stung their eyes as they swung through the library's revolving front door. She couldn't shake the feeling that this particular group of missing books was a sign, a message of some sort that could be decoded.

Edouard's face lit up in that way someone glows when you ask them about the things they love. In Edouard's case, that would be *facts.*

"Fact," he stated matter-of-factly. "Codes are older than language itself."

"What?" Viviani pulled her scarf tighter. "How can that be?"

"Even animals and insects have codes," Edouard said, sidestepping the steam coming from a grate in the sidewalk.

"They do?" Viviani asked with a smile. She knew she'd asked the right person.

"Well, birdsong is a type of code—a language—that birds use. And woodpeckers tapping on wood, that sort of thing. Some think it's for more than just a meal. Also, fireflies."

"Fireflies?"

"Yeah! Entomologists—fact: a person who studies insects is an *entomologist*—anyway, those folks think that when fireflies flash, it's a coded message to potential mates. Like Morse code."

They were at the large, wooden front doors of their school now. Viviani paused, her hand on the cold iron handle.

"But humans had codes and sent secret messages before Samuel Morse invented the telegraph, right?" she asked.

"Yes, the Greeks used to write a message on a clay tablet, then coat the tablet with wax!" Edouard beamed. "When the tablet sat in the sun, the wax melted, and the secret message was revealed."

"Keen!"

"Agreed. I'm trying to figure out how to make invisible ink. I think if I use baking soda, I can write an invisible message on white paper. Perhaps I can find some in the cupboard at home this afternoon . . ." Edouard hurried into the school, leaving Viviani behind.

"Wow." Viviani scanned Forty-Second Street, and maybe for the first time ever, she noticed all the symbols on the buildings around her. Greek key patterns imbedded in brick. Gargoyles looming down from corners.

Flags from a number of countries in store windows. Even the number addresses on the buildings—they each represented a specific location. They might not all be *codes*, but they were patterns, symbols. Things that needed interpretation. Deciphering.

Viviani swung the school door wide, and a blast of heat from inside warmed her cold cheeks. She was convinced more than ever that there was a pattern in those overdue books that she—that *everyone*—was somehow missing.

Dear Friend,

Now I'm not only solving this crime to write this story and win the contest (IF—big IF—it can be solved really fast), but now, more, to save the information inside those rare books.

Sure, I kinda understood before that "knowledge is valuable." But now I really understand: if those books aren't returned, that knowledge is lost forever.

I'm certain there's a clue, a pattern, a code, to these particular books. This story hoarder is telling us something, I'm sure of it. Miss Hutch helped me find a Morse code alphabet in her

books today. If I'm going to crack this code, I
have to start thinking like our story hoarder.

A: ·—   B: ····   C: —·—   D: —··   E: ·
F: ··—·   G: ——   H: ····   I: ··   J: ·———
K: —··   L: ·—··   M: ——   N: —·   O: ———
P: ·——·   Q: ———·   R: ·—·   S: ···   T: —
U: ··—   V: ···—   W: ·——   X: —··—   Y: —·——
Z: ——··

— ···· ·

··· — ——— ·—· —·——

···· ——— ·—· —·— —·· ·—· ·—·

·· ···

···· ·· —··· ·· —· ——·

··· ——— —— · ——— —·· · '···

—·—· ··· —·—· ·—· · !

CHAPTER THIRTEEN

Rare Books—Collectors and Collecting,
Dewey Decimal 016.09

SEE ALSO: *rare books—catalogs; booksellers' catalogs*

"Moppets' meeting!" Viviani declared in the school-yard later that day. She had to shout her declaration over the nearby rattling elevated train. "At the library, after school. We need to learn more about how those overdue books are connected if we want to find those missing texts."

Merit nodded once. "The idea that someone is out there hiding . . . well, *wisdom* that could help someone? I have to admit, that makes me angrier than anything I've seen in a long time!"

"Angrier than a fake ghost?" Eva teased. Two months ago, Viviani had tried to convince Merit ghosts were real by dressing up John Jr. as the library's resident ghost, Big Red. The prank had not gone well.

Merit shot Viviani a look, then chuckled. "Yeah! Even angrier than that!"

As their thoughts all wandered to that night and Big Red, Eva whispered, "You don't suppose . . ."

Viviani shook her head firmly. "Nah, Big Red's already dead. What would he want with a bunch of medical books? It's too late for him."

After school, the three girls dashed through the front door and up the wide steps to the second floor, straight into the administrative offices. ("Slow it *down*, Viviani!") They wound their way through the large room until they reached Miss Schneider's desk.

"We're here to see Mr. Bergquist," Viviani announced. "We'd like to know more about rare books and their value."

Miss Schneider smiled, her fingertips hovering over the typewriter keys, her perfect red lips showcasing a warm smile. "Mr. Bergquist is out right now." She leaned back in her squeaky chair. "Can I answer your questions?"

Viviani grinned. "We just have one: Can you tell us everything?"

Miss Schneider laughed. "Come inside Mr. Bergquist's office. I'll show you instead."

Mr. Bergquist's office was neatish, but there were stacks of old books and empty coffee mugs everywhere.

"Let's see," Miss Schneider said. She sat in Mr. Bergquist's chair and spun side to side slightly. "Well, let's start with the person, shall we?"

Merit and Eva also sat in the guest chairs. Merit dug out her notebook and began scribbling.

"This person isn't just checking out books. He or she is borrowing books that have, well, how to put this? Very little appeal to book collectors. They're valuable, absolutely. But their value is in their content."

"So you don't think those medical books were stolen for money?" Merit asked, looking up from her notes.

Miss Schneider shook her head. "I doubt it." She held up a finger. "Let me show you some of the books we've recently recovered."

Miss Schneider dug a key out from under her blouse that was hanging on a chain around her neck. She unlocked a small metal filing cabinet and hefted a stack of worn, musty books. She placed them gently on Mr. Bergquist's desk, and their smell was unmistakable—*book*. Viviani sniffed, swooned, smiled at the comforting scent.

"Here's a first edition of *Moby-Dick*," Miss Schneider said, flipping the volume over in her hands. "This sold for a thousand dollars to a collector."

Eva whistled long and low.

"And here, this copy of *The Scarlet Letter* also went for a thousand dollars." She picked up a brown clothbound book.

"Wow," Viviani said. She knew she'd grown up around valuable books, but a thousand dollars for *The Scarlet Letter*? That was . . . $3.10 a page!

"And this." Miss Schneider held a worn book up to the light and turned it to and fro, almost reverently. Viviani grinned—she could tell Miss Schneider loved her job and took its responsibilities very seriously. "This is Poe's *Al Aaraaf, Tamerlane, and Minor Poems*."

"Oh, I love Edgar Allan Poe!" Viviani said, joining the reverence.

Miss Schneider smiled. "You're not alone. Only ten copies of this book are thought to exist, and last year a collector paid ten thousand dollars for this book."

"Wow," Merit breathed, so impressed she forgot to take notes. "For one book."

Miss Schneider snapped out of her reverie and locked the valuable books away. "Well, I need to get back to work, girls. I hope you have what you need. We could use all the help we can get on this case."

Miss Schneider winked as she stood up to let the girls out of the office.

"Thank you, Miss Schneider," Viviani said, pumping her hand in a handshake. "The Moppets are on it!"

In the hallway, the friends paused, taking in all they'd learned.

"Well," Merit said at last, "what do we think?"

Viviani scratched her head. "Something's not right, you know? Those books she showed us—they're nothing like the medical texts. I truly feel like there's a pattern we're just not seeing yet . . ." Viviani scratched her chin.

Eva nodded.

Merit fiddled with knobs on her camera. "So what you're saying is, this person isn't like the others?"

"Exactly," Viviani said, rubbing her hands. "He or she isn't taking poetry or stories. This person is hoarding *facts*."

Nothing unlocked Viviani's brain better than her hand pressing ink into paper, so later that afternoon, Viviani recorded some thoughts in her captain's log:

LIST OF MISSING BOOKS IN ALPHABETICAL ORDER

By Viviani Fedeler, Eva Derian, and Merit Mubarak

—*Anaerobic Bacteria: Role in Disease*, checked out January 20, 1929

—*Bacterial and Mycotic Infections of Man*, checked out January 20, 1929

—*Basics of Pharmacology*, checked out January 23, 1929

—<u>Diseases of the Lung</u>, checked out February 2, 1929

—<u>Health Almanac 1920</u>, checked out January 16, 1929

—<u>Modern Advances in Treating Lung Disease</u>,
checked out February 2, 1929

—<u>Pulmonology Cures</u>, checked out February 2, 1929

—<u>Textbook of Bacteriology</u>, checked out January 20, 1929

And, Dear Friend, Miss Hutch has helped me find more ways to encrypt messages! This one is called the Caesar Shift, where each letter is shifted a certain number of places down the alphabet. The key you need here is TWO:

UVQTKGU CTG OKUUKPI GXGTAYJGTG!

K'NN HKPF AQW, YOTFU, K RTQOKUG.

CHAPTER FOURTEEN

Medical Care,

Dewey Decimal 616.02

SEE ALSO: *physician and patient, self-care, health*

Before school the following morning, Viviani was outside petting Leo Lenox's marble mane. Since the Fedeler kids couldn't keep pets in their library home, Viviani liked to think of these lions as her personal feline companions, and she often confided in them.

"What do you think?" Viviani whispered to Lenox. "Do I have enough time to solve this mystery for the essay contest? Or should I come up with another idea? Oh, Lenox. I'm flummoxed."

"Good morning, Vivian!" said a sharp voice. *Vivian?*

Viviani turned, and there was Dr. Monroe, *clickclick-click*ing up the marble stairs into the library. The doctor paused, spun on her heel, looked down the slant of her nose, and asked, "I'm certain you and your brothers have fully recovered from that long list of symptoms you provided my assistant, Benjamin? I trust I would've heard otherwise." The doctor grimaced, her lipstick pulling into a tight red knot on the side of her face.

Viviani gulped. This woman surely had spells and potions of all sorts that could be used to read Viviani's mind. She pictured the doctor pouring them in and out of tiny smoking beakers, uttering spooky phrases like *eye of newt* and *wing of bat*. "Um, yes, ma'am. We're all healthy as a bunch of ox. Uh . . . oxes. *Ahem.* That's what John Jr. says."

Dr. Monroe rolled her eyes. "*Oxen.* And a bunch of oxen is called a *rake*."

"Oh, ha! Like *olly olly oxen free*." Viviani giggled nervously. Why did doctors always flutter her nerves?

Dr. Monroe's eyes narrowed. "I suppose." She spun so quickly on her sharp heel, Viviani was surprised that she didn't leave a tiny hole drilled in the marble, smoke drifting up. Dr. Monroe marched up the stairs and continued into the library.

Viviani gulped again—a double-gulper of a conversation, this was! "That woman terrifies me," she whispered to Lenox. "If she weren't a doctor—"

Wait!

A *doctor*!

Why was she here doing research if Benjamin was already here researching for her?

Could she be a suspect? Checking out medical texts and not returning them?

Ab-so-*lutely*.

Viviani decided to trail her and see where she was headed, even if she'd be a bit late for school. But she had to be careful, of course. It would be awful to be on the bad side of a woman with Dr. Monroe's powers.

She raced up the stairs, following the *clickclickclick* of heels before spotting the doctor in the crowd, whirling into the library through the revolving front door.

Viviani ducked here and there, stooping behind a woman in a wheelchair, then shadowing a gentleman with a tall, dark hat, then diving into a coatrack. She kept Dr. Monroe in her sights, watching her start up the staircase, until . . .

"Five points, Viviani!" Mr. Eames shouted across the echoing main hall. The night guard was headed home after his nocturnal shift. "You're losing your touch! I spotted you hiding in that coatrack from across the room!"

Viviani peeked out from behind the row of coats.

Dr. Monroe had paused and was glaring at her from the stairwell. She shook her head ever so slightly, turned again on that heel of hers, and stalked away.

Viviani felt frustration punch around inside her stomach. She'd been spotted—and by scary Dr. Monroe, no less!

Viviani looked up from her crouch behind the coats, directly into the beady black eyes of a fox stole, strewn limply across a hanger.

"What are you looking at?" she asked with a shudder.

Dear Friend,

Oh my, what a day! After I followed Dr. Monroe in the library, I tried to turn the caper into a friendship story. It was abysmal. Heavens. I have two days to catch a tale of friendship by the tail and wrangle it onto the page. I'm certainly not going to get there penning stories titled "Dr. Witch, the Witch Doctor"! At this point, I am sure I'm going to lose my family's story collector status. Perhaps they'll merely demote me to word watcher, rather than strip me of all story honors altogether.

And worse? The library now thinks MORE BOOKS are missing! More medical texts and other books have been checked out using fake names and addresses that lead to dry cleaners and bath houses. The librarians believe the following titles are now part of the story hoarder's collection:

—*Anatomy and Physiology*, checked out
February 3, 1929

—*The Blessing of Death*, checked out
February 7, 1929

—*Greeting Death with Peace and Dignity*,
checked out, February 7, 1929

Today's code is one Edouard came up with. He calls it the Typewriter Code because it's made by shifting your fingertips on a typewriter one space to the right so that instead of A, you would type the next key to the right, S; instead of B, you'd write N, and so

on. John Jr. wouldn't stop teasing me when
we discovered my name in code would be...
Bobosmo!

With that...

O eo;; gomf upi. ,oddomh dyptord

CHAPTER FIFTEEN

Inspiration,

Dewey Decimal 153.3

SEE ALSO: *creative ability, courage*

Viviani felt the essay deadline creeping up on her like Big Red, the ghost rumored to wander the stacks of the library. And here she was, with no answers whatsoever to the mystery. Would she have to write a different story? She didn't want to; she didn't *have* another story.

"I need inspiration," Viviani told Eva and Merit the next afternoon in the schoolyard. "The essay is due tomorrow! I was planning to write about how the Moppets solved another mystery, but now it seems like our overdue books won't be found in time. And I'm positively storyless!"

"Storyless," Merit repeated. She still questioned when Viviani and Eva took it upon themselves to better the English language by making up a new word.

"I am *sans* yarn!" Viviani said, laying the back of her hand against her forehead dramatically. "I am lacking in legend! I am devoid of narrative! I AM A GIRL WITHOUT WORDS!"

Merit chuckled. "You are far from that."

Viviani grinned, too. "Honestly. What should I do?"

Eva twirled a dark curl around her finger. "Why don't you revisit some of your earlier ideas and see if they inspire you now?"

Viviani nodded, sighed. "I'll try that."

Viviani headed back to the library. The room that had interested Viviani the most lately was, of course, the Rare Books Room. So up the stairs she went, into the Main Reading Room, and *knock, knock!* The door was unlocked, and in she went into the Rare Books Room. She inhaled books. Aaaaaah!

Miss Fillipelli smiled. "What can I do for you, Viviani?"

Viviani thought back to when she and Edouard had visited this room last week. The book they'd studied that day was fascinating—all those muscles and bones and tissues connecting everything. Miss Bones, dancing across the old, yellowed pages. Perhaps that would provide her with more inspiration.

"I'd like to see *Cunningham's Text-book of Anatomy* again please, Miss Fillipelli."

The librarian nodded and drifted toward the medical books, up a set of stairs and in a corner. She ran her fingertips lightly over the ancient book spines until—

"Oh!" Miss Fillipelli said. "It appears to be checked out."

She returned to her desk and flipped through her check-out cards. "It is. It's checked out. And the books here can only be checked out for a day, which means it's overdue." Miss Fillipelli looked at Viviani with wide eyes. "You don't suppose . . ."

Viviani nodded curtly. "I do, Miss Fillipelli. I think this book should be added to our list. Miss Bones is now a *missing person*."

Viviani made her way to the map room for her lesson with Mr. Green. She was early, so she flipped open her captain's log and began writing:

Dear Friend,

I am so angry! The anatomy book that Edouard and I are fond of—the one with Miss Bones—is now one of the missing overdue books! I think I know EXACTLY who it is. Oh, when the Moppets and I catch you, Dr. Story Hoarder, you'd better watch out!

"Ahem!" Mr. Green said.

Viviani jumped. "You do that every time!"

"I tried not to. I cleared me throat jest for that purpose. Don't blame me if the girl can't hear."

Viviani slumped in her chair. "Sorry, Mr. Green. It's, well . . . there's another book missing. They discovered it was overdue just this afternoon."

Mr. Green's scowl got scowlier. "I'd like to catch the rat who's doing this meself."

Viviani grinned and thought of the mysterious custodial closet where Mr. Green stored all his supplies. She used to imagine he kept instruments of torture and all sorts of acids and poisons in there. Now she imagined that Mr. Green would simply scowl at this story hoarder until he confessed. "Are we ready for our lesson?"

Mr. Green plunked a wrinkly paper bag on the table and pulled out *Millions of Cats*.

Viviani drummed her fingertips on the wide oak table. "Again?"

Mr. Green chuckled. "I like the very old man and the very old woman. It's like them two are friends, 'steada married."

"Friends?" Viviani said, sitting up straighter.

"Well, yeah." Mr. Green pointed at the carved-wood illustrations: the man and his puffing pipe, the woman in her wide kerchief. "I like their friendship."

Viviani's head swirled with thoughts: *this* was a story

about friendship! And it must have millions of readers. Billions and trillions of readers. She stood, threw her arms about Mr. Green. His shoulders stiffened. "Oh, thank you, Mr. Green! When I win this essay contest and my story gets printed in the *Times*, I'll be sure to let them know *you* were my inspiration."

Viviani dashed out of the room, Mr. Green muttering behind her, "Well, now, I guess you're welcome."

CHAPTER SIXTEEN

Fiction Authorship,
Dewey Decimal 808.3

SEE ALSO: *creative writing, literature*

M illions of Cats!
Viviani must've read that story a hundred times, a thousand times, a million, billion, trillion times with Mr. Green, and there it was, leaping off the picture book pages at her: a perfect story of friendship. The very old man, the very old woman, and their kitten.

Viviani put pen to paper, and the words flowed like the glittering tail of a comet from her pen nib. This was no just-in-case story, Viviani knew. This was the story she was supposed to tell all along. Elements from her recent days found their way into this tale: codes and friendship and finding things. It felt as if this story had been suspended out in the universe, just waiting for Viviani to pluck it like an apple that was finally ripe.

That was Viviani's favorite part of writing: when it went well, she felt like she disappeared. The story would gush out of her fingertips, weaving a world from nothing more than ink on paper, yet spun of everything important: emotions and people and relationships and pain and longing and love. Characters would make her laugh. Make her cry. Surprise her and outrage her.

Have you ever felt that, Dear Friend? *That* is the magic of writing at its best—it feels like you are channeling it rather than creating it. Like the story already exists, and you just have to crack open your heart wide enough to set it free.

Viviani turned in her essay the next morning. She'd learned something about being a writer: it often wasn't the first or second or third or even fourth idea that was the best idea. But she was confident that *this* story—even though it wasn't a solved Moppets mystery—was good enough to win and cement her legacy as a true story collector. A story*teller*. Viviani grinned and winked at Miss Hutch. Miss Hutch grinned and winked back.

Viviani was filled with smiles. Hundreds of smiles. Thousands of smiles. Millions and billions and trillions of smiles.

CHAPTER SEVENTEEN

Machines,

Dewey Decimal 621.8

SEE ALSO: *simple machines, machinery—history*

L ater that day in class, Viviani wrote a note to Merit and Eva: *Meet at the library after school.* Now that Viviani's essay was turned in, she and the Moppets were free to solve this mystery. Viviani knew that there had to be a pattern to the overdue books that they weren't seeing. Maybe it was even a code hidden in the titles of the overdue books . . .

Miss Hutch frowned when she caught Viviani slipping her note into Eva's palm. "Is there something you'd like to share with the class, Viviani?"

Viviani gulped. "Uh, sure, Miss Hutch! I invited Eva and Merit to meet me at the library after school. Everyone here is welcome at the library. Always."

Miss Hutch *almost* smiled at that, Viviani could tell.

After school, the girls raced up the stairs ("Slow it *down*, Viviani!"), into the rotunda, through the catalog room, into the Main Reading Room, and through the doors *knock! unlock!* of the Rare Books Room.

"It's time to go straight to the people! Let's ask the patrons if they know anything," Viviani whispered loudly. She lifted her chin at the camera swinging from Merit's neck. "Can you take pictures without the flash?"

Merit scanned the room: the two-story bookshelves, the stairs, the overhead lighting, the dark, musty books. "Sure. But there are no windows in this room, so they'll likely come out too dark."

Eva's brow wrinkled. "We need photographic evidence! That's what solved the mystery last time."

Viviani stroked her chin. "We'll try our hardest."

The girls fanned out in the cozy room, Viviani breathing in the scent of books on shelves like flowers in garden rows. Viviani and Eva talked to several patrons in hushed tones: "Have you seen anything odd?" "So . . . check out any good books lately?" "Will you let us know if you do?" Merit snapped quiet photos of the shelves, the books.

Viviani was getting nowhere. She scanned the room, and—"Hello again!" There, hunched over one of the wide oak tables, was the fellow from Dr. Monroe's office. "Benjamin!"

The fellow looked up, his eyes buggy behind his thick

glasses. He smiled. "Hello! Good to see you again, Edouard!"

Viviani giggled and dropped into a carved chair opposite him. "Hey, maybe you can help us. There are a few more missing books from this room lately. Have you seen any—"

"You CANNOT take photos in here, Miss Mubarak!"

Merit shook her head and stammered, "I—I wasn't using a flash! Honest, Miss Fillipelli!"

Miss Fillipelli's nostrils flared, and she shook her head so rapidly, Viviani wondered how she wasn't dizzy. "No. No. I have some very valuable books that aren't being returned. The least I can do is protect the ones that are still on our shelves. Dr. Anderson doesn't want to restrict the books that can be checked out, but that is indeed the next step. Viviani, friends—OUT!"

The trio of girls dragged their feet, then huddled outside the door of the Rare Books Room, at a table in the Main Reading Room.

"Do you think you got any photos?" Viviani whispered to Merit.

Merit shrugged. "Maybe a few. I've got twenty photos left on this roll of film, though."

Viviani stood, ran her fingers lightly around the intricate pink marble doorframe of the Rare Books Room. It was cool to the touch. On the other side of this locked door, thousands of rare books sat on shelves, in danger of going missing one by one, their facts lost like forgotten memories.

What the Moppets needed to know most was who was coming and going from this room.

Viviani stepped back, studying the doorframe, the elaborate iron wall sconces on either side of the entry. She backed up farther to get a better view and tripped over her own shoe. She toppled to the floor.

"Shhhhh!" hushed a librarian from who knows where. That was one of the librarians' special powers— instantaneous, invisible shushes.

From her crumpled position, Viviani could see the situation from a new angle. "You know what we need, friends?"

Eva shook her head as Merit pulled Viv off the cool marble floor. Viv dusted herself off.

"We need a way to take pictures of everyone who comes and goes from this room. Discreetly."

"But how?" Merit asked. "There's no way I could wait out here with my camera all day."

Viviani sighed. "If only we had a camera that could take photographs without a photographer to push the button . . ."

Eva nodded fervently. "Oh! I have an idea. I've been studying these cartoons—drawn by a fellow named Rube Goldberg. He invents these silly machines . . . well, here. It's easier if I just show you. Follow me!"

Viviani's eyes gleamed as she and Merit followed Eva down two flights of stairs. Eva was usually the careful one, so when she hatched a plan, Viviani *knew* it would be good.

The girls continued through the long hallway and down a couple flights of stairs to the opposite end of the building, swinging through the heavy oak doors of the Periodical Reading Room. The librarian helped them find a copy of the *Chicago Tribune*, and Eva flipped through the newspaper until she found what she was seeking: a cartoon titled NO MORE OVERSLEEPING.

The drawing featured a man asleep on a bed, under a window. Around him was a contraption involving containers of water and bowling balls and levers and pulleys, all designed to be set in motion when the sun rose and sent a ray of light through a magnifying glass. Once activated, the bed tilted up and plopped the man directly into his shoes, prepping him for the day. The Moppets could hardly contain their giggles, looking at this silly thing.

Viviani ran her fingers over the newsprint. This room was the opposite of the Rare Books Room—here, you were encouraged to touch, to handle, to flip, to read. The girls looked at a few other Goldberg cartoons. The drawings were hysterical—each of them a tangle of contraptions designed to do something as simple as wipe your face with a napkin or peel the shell off a hardboiled egg.

Viviani slowly smiled. So did Merit and Eva.

"Eva, this is brilliant. This is *exactly* what we should build to take that photo and see if we can catch our story hoarder on film. And if we're building a Rube Goldberg mechanism, you know who we need?"

Merit and Eva nodded and said in unison, "John Jr."

CHAPTER EIGHTEEN

Pulleys,

Dewey Decimal 621.8

SEE ALSO: *levers, simple machines*

After the library closed that evening, Viviani brought John Jr. to the entryway of the Rare Books Room to map out her idea. The door to the room was locked tight for the night, so there would be no entering it now. (And only a handful of people likely had keys to the room: Miss Fillipelli and Papa, certainly. Dr. Anderson, probably. Possibly Mr. Green, but Viviani had a better chance of sprouting wings and flying than getting him to unlock this door after hours.)

John Jr. paced the floor of the reading room, scratching his chin and muttering, "Hmmm. I see." *Clack clack clack* went his loafers against the red tile floor. "Maybe . . ."

He paused suddenly and pointed at Viviani. "Write this down."

Viviani flipped open her captain's log and uncapped her pen.

List of Supplies for Operation "Gotcha, Story Hoarder!"

—twine, sturdy but not too thick

—two pulleys, "make sure one of them is a double pulley"

—a ~~3-pound~~ no, a 6-pound weight

—a can of grease

"And that should do 'er," John Jr. said smugly. He nodded once. "Meet you here after school tomorrow." And off he stalked, not the least bit nonplussed by this assignment.

Now what you might be thinking, Dear Friend, is how in the world does one find, say, a double pulley lying about? Well, fortunately for Viviani and her mystery-loving pals, her father, superintendent of the library, inventor extraordinaire, and friend of Thomas Edison, happened to have a very well-stocked, if tremendously messy, workshop. *Un*fortunately for Viviani and her mystery-loving pals, said workshop was in the basement.

And her father's workshop, well . . . it was supposed to be off-limits to Viviani. But Viviani had what one might call a sliding sense of "off-limits." Off-limits for hide-and-seek? Sure, all right. Off-limits for a list of supplies that would surely nab the story hoarder and find those rare books? Well, *that* was worth risking any punishment.

Viviani crept down the stairs to the second floor, then the first, then the basement. It was dark here now, and the few dim bulbs threw long shadows on the walls and floors. Viviani tiptoed down the echoing hallway, between the rows of metal staff lockers.

This part of the basement was cold and dark, with an eerie dripping sound bouncing off the stone walls—*drip, drip, drip.* The sound brought to Viviani's mind the idea of pooling blood. She shivered and thought of the ghost, Big Red. They had *never* quite proved he *didn't* exist. She shivered again.

The basement was, in fact, where an old city reservoir once sat. The walls were from the old basin, and so had a chiseled, cave-like look to them, worn by years of holding water prior to their years of bolstering books.

Viviani opened a heavy metal door and turned down the short hall to her father's workshop. This hall was lined with broken furniture and moldings, awaiting Papa's attention. The maze of pipes above her gave a sudden *hiss!* and her skeleton practically leapt out of her skin. The thought of it made her remember Miss Bones, now missing, which renewed her purpose. *Almost there . . .*

Just before entering the workshop, Viviani passed the fiery boiler room, through a hissing blast of dry heat. It had the distinct chalky smell of coal, and the air felt gritty and full of darkness in this spot. It was the coal dust, Viviani knew, but it felt like walking through a grimy midnight hour.

"'Once upon a midnight dreary, while I pondered, weak and weary,'" Viviani recited to herself. It was her favorite Edgar Allan Poe piece, a poem called "The Raven." The creepy basement always made Viviani think of Poe and his famously spooky tales.

She reached the workshop at last and flipped the switch to the solitary lightbulb swaying overhead. *How is it swaying*, Viviani thought, *when this is a windowless, windless basement?* She swallowed hard, then told her imagination to *hush up already, willya?!*

Inside the workshop were saws and rakes and drills and metal contraptions galore, all made creepier by the shadows that seemed to double their size. Viviani tiptoed past tins of Bakelite and rows of screwdrivers and cardboard boxes marked GEARS and SPRINGS. At last, she found the box marked PULLEYS and heaved it, noisily, to the worktable. It landed with a crash.

"Shhhh!" Viviani said, then laughed. "Now I'm shushing myself," she whispered. "You win, librarians! You hear that? *You win! I'm now shushing myself!*"

Viviani dug through the clattery, clangy box and

quickly found two pulleys, one with double wheels and one with a single wheel. There was a variety of twine to choose from—spools and spools—so she chose one that was relatively light and invisible but strong, like fishing line. There were also multiple cans of grease; Viviani grabbed a brass canister, halfway full. And the weights that counterbalanced all the dumbwaiters in the building were lined up like soldiers reporting for duty. Viviani checked the bottom of each one until she found a six-pounder. "Well, you're heavier than you look, soldier!" she said, and pocketed it with the rest of her loot. It weighed her dress down like an anchor.

"All set," Viviani said, and she crept out of the workshop, clicking off the light behind her. As she passed the boiler room, the furnace clanged awake, fiery and puffing. Viviani yelped.

"'Tis some visitor,' I muttered, . . . 'Only this and nothing more.'" She quoted more Poe to distract herself, but it had the opposite effect. It didn't lift Viviani's spirits a bit, thinking of a *visitor*, someone else down here in the basement with her. She hustled up two flights of stairs and into her family's bright, cheery apartment, her pockets jangling with contraband.

CHAPTER NINETEEN

Bees,

Dewey Decimal 638.1

SEE ALSO: *bees—guidebooks; beekeeping*

Viviani felt as buzzy as a hive of bees the next day at school.

"I've got everything we need," she whispered to Eva and Merit as she slid into her seat. She tapped her foot impatiently as Miss Hutch started class. She was so excited to get home and have John Jr. help her with her Rube Goldberg contraption. Con*trap*tion. They'd trap that story hoarder for sure! Oh, how wonderful that those two words hugged each other like that! Viviani loved words whose meanings sang in harmony.

Miss Hutch straightened the stack of papers she held, *tap tap tap*ping their edges into a neat pile.

Jittery bees were still buzzing around inside Viviani's

head, so much so that she barely heard her teacher say, "Class, I've selected a winner for the essay contest."

Viviani sat up, heart pounding. She had forgotten that today was the day Miss Hutch would announce the winner. She held her breath, shooting a nervous glance at Merit and Eva.

"Congratulations, Viviani Fedeler!"

"I won?" Viviani said, blinking. She totally forgot to pull the *I won?* face she'd been practicing all week in the bathroom mirror, before she even had *the* story idea. Both Merit and Eva turned to her and beamed, and Eva shot her a discreet double thumbs-up.

Viviani smiled back, and her jitters bubbled up and evaporated, fizzing and popping away like the bubbles over a Moxie soda.

"And, class, I'm going to ask Viviani to duplicate a copy of her story for each one of you. It will be a part of your memorization and recitation grade." Viviani's classmates groaned, but Viviani grinned.

"I won!"

She was going to the *New York Times*! Her words would be in print! She was indeed a true story collector. A story sharer. A storyteller.

CHAPTER TWENTY

Trapping Equipment and Supplies,

Dewey Decimal 639.1

SEE ALSO: *traps, snares*

That afternoon, Viviani floated home and met her friends inside the Main Reading Room. *I won!* Viviani smiled up at the blue-sky ceiling. *I really WON. I'm a story collector. A storyteller! An actual* writer*! And soon my story will appear in print. In the NEW. YORK. TIMES!*

It was all going according to plan. Now she just needed to track down the person hoarding all those valuable medical texts. Even though she was about to launch her career as a star reporter, the library still came first. So Viviani and the Moppets moved ahead with the Rube Goldberg con*trap*tion.

John Jr. knocked to be let into the Rare Books Room. He had a stepladder strung over one shoulder and the can of grease in his hand. Viviani, Eva, and Merit hid around the corner of the doorframe.

"Routine maintenance, ma'am," John Jr. told Miss Fillipelli when she unlocked the door. "Helping my pa oil the doorjambs today."

Miss Fillipelli waved her hand at the door absently. "Have at it."

Viviani peered around the corner as the door closed almost completely behind her brother; he left it open just a smidge so it wouldn't lock. Viviani and the Moppets didn't follow him in; they had pushed Miss Fillipelli to the limit yesterday, and they didn't want to arouse further suspicion. Viviani imagined what John Jr. was doing inside, according to the plan: it *looked* like he was pumping oil onto the hinges of the door (which he would actually do, of course—there had to be *some* truth to the plan to offset the sneaky parts). But he was also threading the twine around the metal mechanism attached to the inside top of the door. It was an elbow of sorts, this mechanism; each door in the library had one. They helped the doors ease shut slowly and silently, keeping the quiet, studious library slam-free.

The door opened wider, and the skein of twine flew out, unraveling—*whirrrrrr!*—in midair. Eva chased it down.

"Thanks, Miss F!" John Jr. called over his shoulder. Once the door to the Rare Books Room locked behind him, he propped the stepladder near the wall sconce and climbed up. John Jr. helped Papa enough around the library that the staff would assume he was changing out a lightbulb.

"Double pulley," John Jr. whispered like a surgeon at the operating table, and held out his hand. Viviani dug the pulley from her pocket. He hooked it onto the sconce.

"Twine," he said. Eva handed him the skein. He eyed the doorframe, the nearest table—the whole setup—and measured three quick chest-to-fingertip lengths. He gnawed the twine with his teeth, then threaded it through one wheel of the double pulley.

"Single pulley." Viviani handed it to him, and he threaded that on the twine, too, about eighteen inches below the original pulley. He then pulled the twine over the second wheel in the double-pulley and tied the six-pound weight on the end.

"There!" he said, hopping from the stepladder, dusting off his hands. "Now, when someone opens the door, A"—he pointed to the twine threaded over the top of the door—"the pulleys, B and C, will rotate. The weight, D, will then lower and push the button on E, Merit's camera. Where is it?"

Merit hesitantly looped the camera off her neck. "You're *sure* nothing will happen to this?"

"We're sure," Viviani and John Jr. said simultaneously.

Viviani did a quick calculation of how many hours of chores she'd need to do if, say, something *did* happen and she had to pay for a new one. Which she wouldn't. Probably.

Eva dragged a heavy carved chair over from one of the study tables in the reading room, putting it as close to the sconce as possible without making it look too out of place.

Merit stepped back, eyeing the situation. "If we set the camera on the seat of the chair, we'll end up with a lot of pictures of kneecaps and belt buckles."

Viviani pulled seven, then eight, books off a nearby shelf, placing the camera on top. Merit nodded once. "That'll do it."

"Okay, watch how it works." John Jr. knocked on the door again. The girls ducked behind the doorframe, peering around the corner. The leather-covered door to the Rare Books Room swung open, and the twine whirred smoothly around the pulleys, lowering the weight. But oh! The weight swayed so much when lowered that it missed the camera completely, swung back, clonked it, and practically knocked it off its book stack. Eva discreetly caught the falling camera before it tumbled to the floor. Merit gasped. Viviani's eyes widened, but she quickly shushed her friend—they had to stay quiet!

Miss Fillipelli raised a single eyebrow when she saw it was John again.

"Left a tool inside. Sorry—I'll only be a sec."

He ducked inside. The girls waited, watching carefully for the door to open again. The handle rattled as the door was unlocked from the inside. The door opened, and the pulleys whirred through the mechanism again.

"Huh. Don't know where I left it, then," John Jr. said over his shoulder, back into the Rare Books Room. "Thanks anyway, Miss F!"

"I have an idea," Eva whispered.

Once the door closed, she scooped up the empty umbrella rack that stood beside the door, the one Viviani had tripped over just the day before. It was brass, open on all sides: a grid of metal made to hold multiple umbrellas. Eva balanced the stand atop the books atop the chair. It was tall and teetering, but it stood.

Merit sighed, then placed her dear camera gingerly inside the bottom of the stand. Eva laced the six-pound weight through one of the holes at the top of the umbrella stand.

"There," she declared. "The umbrella stand should stop the weight from swaying so much on the string."

Viviani grinned. "Let's try it! John?"

John Jr. knocked again; again the girls ducked out of view. The door eased open, the pulleys whirred, the weight lowered inside the umbrella stand, and *click!* landed perfectly on the shutter button of Merit's camera.

The girls clapped hands over their mouths to contain squeals. John Jr. pumped his fist. "Yes!"

But Miss Fillipelli looked positively perturbed at unlocking the door only to find him there again. He flashed his *forgive me* smile. (He'd long ago perfected that one.)

"One last thing I forgot, Miss F. So sorry."

He started to walk through the door, paused, patted himself theatrically, and spun back around. "Oh! Never mind, Miss F! Found what I was looking for right here in my pocket!"

The door closed but not before they heard Miss Fillipelli grumbling, "Lock the door, unlock the door. Lock the door, unlock the door. No wonder the hinges need greasing."

John Jr. beamed at this Rube Goldberg contraption, then turned his smile to Eva. "Hey, listen. You ever need a mentor when it comes to mischief, you keep me in mind, okay?"

"Viviani. John."

Viviani and John Jr. exchanged an *uh-oh* look at the stern sound of Papa's loud whisper, drifting to them across the Main Reading Room. They shifted to block their invention from his line of vision. But instead of

Papa marching forward and asking *What in the dickens is going on here?*, he waved at them.

"Come."

Merit and Eva exchanged a quick *let's get out of here before the punishments begin* glance. With sympathetic shrugs, they turned and scooted home.

Outside, in the rotunda, Mama and Edouard waited. Viviani got a lump in her throat. Hoo boy, they hadn't even had the chance to put their plan in action. She and John Jr. had apparently just set a land speed record for getting into big trouble. But Mama wasn't ticking her foot, and Edouard wasn't shooting them discreet *What did you do now?* glances. Huh.

Papa took Viviani's hand. "Come on," he said.

The Fedelers wound their way to the first floor of the library and toward the back of the building, through the door marked STAFF ONLY and into the dark, quiet area that housed the seven-story bookshelves.

The sun was low, and the long windows in this part of the building faced west, so great swaths of golden light filled the whole area. At this time of day, there were only a few staff members tiptoeing up and down the metal stairs, reshelving returns for the next day's patrons. Papa and Viviani went up one, two, three short flights of metal stairs, with the rest of the clan following behind. He stopped in front of an aisle marked FICTION: FA–FI.

Papa ran his pointer finger along the dusty shelf ("We gotta get Mr. Green in here") until he found the one spot he was seeking in eighty-five miles of shelves. He stuck his finger between two volumes, *Mosquitoes* by William Faulkner and *The Great Gatsby* by F. Scott Fitzgerald.

"Here, Firecracker!" he said, breaking into a huge smile. "Here is where your book will sit someday. Congratulations on winning the essay contest! Edouard told us all about it. Of course they picked yours. You're a real storyteller now!"

Mama kissed Viviani and left a huge coral smear of lipstick on her cheek. "You did it, hon."

John Jr. put her in a headlock and tickled her. "You didn't say a word, Red! I would've been crowing about it all day long."

"Uncle!" Viviani cried through laughter. "Uncle!"

And Edouard said, "Fact: the *New York Times* has approximately seven hundred fifty thousand readers on Sundays."

Three quarters of a million! Viviani's heart exploded into just as many pieces, she was certain.

Viviani looked at the trail Papa's finger had blazed through the dust. The trail that led directly to *her spot* on the shelves. Her eyes prickled.

And that, Dear Friend, is how Viviani grew misty-eyed over a blank space.

CHAPTER TWENTY-ONE

Publishing,

Dewey Decimal 808.02

SEE ALSO: *authors and publishers, publishers and publishing*

"**V**iviani Joffre Fedeler!"

There it was: Viviani's full name, shouted down the long hallway of their eight-room apartment. Viviani's full name was special to her, unique. She was named for two French dignitaries: the former prime minister Viviani and Marshal Joffre, who had visited the library as Great War allies in 1917, just two days after she was born in this very building. Mama and Papa had struggled to find the perfect moniker for their zesty, red-haired newborn, so when those two important men with their two important names strolled the wide marble halls, her parents landed upon the perfect title for *her* story.

"Viviani Joffre Fedeler, where are you?"

But as any kid knows, when parents use their child's full name, it means trouble. Every kid's middle name might as well be *You're About to Get It*. Viviani You're-About-to-Get-It Fedeler. Accurate.

"In here," Viviani said from the bathroom, her voice echoing. She'd been practicing her *who, me?* faces for when she'd surely be asked for an autograph at the *Times* offices: fingertips on chest, eyebrows raised, mouth in a tiny, round O. *Who, me? Sign your copy of my essay? Why, certainly. And I'd like to take this moment to thank Miss Hutch. I couldn't have done it without her excellent tutelage.* Viviani clutched a wide paddle hairbrush to her heart like a trophy.

Mama stood outside the closed door. "Can I come in?"

"Am I in trouble?"

"You're not on easy street, kid."

The door swung wide. Mama paused, then cracked a grin when she saw Viviani on a step stool, clutching a hairbrush like a treasured award. But Viviani's middle name was You're-About-to-Get-It, so Mama scrambled the look on her face back to *perturbed*.

"What is all this?" Mama held Merit's camera in one hand, a jumble of twine and pulleys in the other.

"An invention?" Viviani answered. This was usually an excellent answer to provide, as Papa was an inventor, too, and Viviani's parents prized a pastime that prioritized imagination. "I . . . uh . . . built it this afternoon."

"Do you want to hear about how Miss Fillipelli ended up tangled in this . . . *invention* and had to be cut free with scissors by her assistant?"

Do NOT laugh at that image, Viviani told herself, mashing her knuckles against her lips. *Do NOT picture Miss Fillipelli as a large spider lurking in her web . . .*

"Viviani! This isn't funny!"

Viviani sucked her lips as far into her face as they could go. Her eyes watered because her laughter had to escape somehow. She nodded.

Mama knitted her eyebrows together.

"All right, it's a little funny," she whispered, grinning. "But! You can't go stringing up contraptions like this, Viviani. Miss Fillipelli got very snarled in this. Imagine if a patron had gotten tangled in this mess."

"Sorry, ma'am." She nodded. "Is Merit's camera okay?"

Mama flipped it to and fro in her hand. "Appears to be." She handed the camera to Viviani. "I'm sure she'll be eager to have it back. No more traps, you hear?"

Mama turned to leave. Viviani's heart leapt. That was it? Was there no punish—

"Oh, and you have extra chores for a week, kiddo. Starting tonight."

"But I can't tonight! I have to copy my assignment onto that ditto stencil Miss Hutch gave me! My story's getting published in school tomorrow."

Mama smiled. "Published, huh? All right, then. Chores first thing tomorrow morning."

There it was. The *You're About to Get It* became the *You Got It.*

As it turned out, a ditto stencil was actually a small stack of waxy paper bound together, one of the sheets coated in black ink. Per Miss Hutch's instructions, Viviani pressed down as hard as she could with her pencil, careful not to poke through the paper. The ink would bleed up through the stack of waxy paper, creating a stencil that would be used to make copies.

Viviani quickly got a hand cramp from pressing down so hard, but she said, "'Tis the price a bard pays to share her stories!" She giggled, swiped her brow, and got back to work.

A few times, she messed up a word and had to block out her misspelling. Her lines were a bit of a mess, too, skewing upward at the end like the words were lifting off into the skies. It was so much harder to write on unlined paper!

But eventually she reached *The End* and sat back,

running her sore fingers up and down her arms, admiring her soon-to-be-duplicated words.

She skipped down to dinner ("Liver again? Ugh!"), and when she dropped into her seat, Papa laughed. "Did you get into a fistfight with a squid, Firecracker?"

"And lose?" John Jr. added with a chuckle.

Viviani looked at her fingers, her arms. Covered in black ink!

"Your cheeks, too," Edouard said, mouth full.

Mama sighed. "Go wash up, Viv."

But no amount of scrubbing at the kitchen sink would budge those stubborn ink stains. Viviani didn't mind—ink-stained fingers were a symbol of a true writer! Mama wasn't nearly as understanding.

"Eat, and we'll get it off later."

After dinner, Mama tried everything: rubbing alcohol, which smelled like Dr. Monroe's office and made Viviani's stomach flop. Harsh lye soap, which smelled like smoky ammonia. More ugh. More floppy stomach. Scrubbing, scrubbing, scrubbing. Viviani's skin turned raw and red, but the ink had faded only a tad.

Mama sat back and sighed. Then she smiled. "You do look like a writer, covered in ink, you know."

Viviani beamed. "I think so, too."

Mama kissed her reddened, smudged cheek. "Your words are going to change the world, kiddo."

"You think so, Mama?"

"I do."

Viviani had never felt more like a true story collector than she did at that very moment.

CHAPTER TWENTY-TWO

Chores,

Dewey Decimal 331

SEE ALSO: *jobs, responsibilities, work*

The next morning, it was time for Viviani's punishment for the con*trap*tion. Fortunately, the penalty
was something she secretly loved: helping Papa around
the library. Sure, she dragged her toes and mumbled a
lot because if her parents were to discover that she
actually *enjoyed* her punishment, they'd find something
else, something terrible, for her to do. Like needle-
point. Or knitting. Ugh. The only downside? She had
to get up *so early*. But this particular morning, she had
no trouble popping up from bed. After all, it was the
day her story would make its publishing debut in her
classroom!

"Let's go, Firecracker!" Papa said, and Viviani yawned

and hefted the long wooden box stuffed with tools. "We've got a lot of fixing ahead of us this morning."

They changed out lightbulbs—teeny, tiny ones—in the small, hot lamps that shone on the paintings in the Stuart Gallery. They replaced lengths of electrical wire in the administrative offices on the second floor, blowing on thin wisps of copper, twisting them together until—*voilà!*—"let there be light!" They fixed a wobbly leg on a podium and returned it to the exhibition room.

"I hear your contraption for snapping pictures was pretty sophisticated," Papa said as they headed back toward the basement to stoke the furnace.

Viviani cleared her throat. She didn't want to rat out John Jr. for helping. "Yes, I hope we got some good shots," she said, easing the subject in a different direction. "When we catch that story hoarder, I'm going to give him the what-for. I've got a real beef with that bum. So greedy!" *Holding Miss Bones hostage and all* . . .

Papa chuckled. "I don't doubt it," he said. "Just remember, Firecracker, that sometimes people who make bad choices have their reasons. They aren't all evil."

"How do you mean?"

"Well, think of King Midas, one of the greediest fellows in fiction," Papa said.

"The golden touch." Viviani nodded, then sniffed.

"Egomaniac. It backfired on him, too. He turned his daughter to gold."

Papa chuckled and spun a wrench in his hand. "Yes, exactly. But he wasn't evil—we saw that in how he grieved the loss of his daughter. Bad choices almost always backfire, my love. Sometimes sooner, sometimes later. And consider this: very few folks wake up and say, 'I believe I'll do something awful today.' They're usually driven by desperation."

Viviani must've looked skeptical, because Papa continued:

"'Neither a borrower nor a lender be,' Firecracker. You know who said that?"

"Of course," Viviani said. "Your favorite, Shakespeare. Solid advice, wouldn't you say?"

"Hmm. What if libraries lived by that policy?" Papa sighed. "Would they still be as valuable?"

They entered the furnace room, and Papa flung open the door of the massive heater. A blast of hot, dry air made Viviani blink, squint. Papa shoveled black, dusty coal into the pit, and the flames leapt up to eat it.

"Surely you aren't saying that this story hoarding is okay?" Viviani said, her words evaporating in the heat of this room.

Papa clanged the door of the furnace shut and turned the iron latch to secure it. "Not at all, Firecracker. But

147

there might be more than meets the eye. And you of all people know that everyone has a story to share. My prizewinning storyteller!" He smiled gently and mopped the sweat and coal dust off his face with a dirty handkerchief.

"Maybe our fella is hoarding stories because he's desperately seeking a happy ending."

CHAPTER TWENTY-THREE

Plagiarism,
Dewey Decimal 808

SEE ALSO: *piracy (copyright)*, *copyright infringement*

Viviani raced to school after finishing up her early-morning chores with Papa. Because today, Viviani Joffre Fedeler would become a published author! Miss Hutch had made her story an assignment for the *whole class*—they would have to memorize Viviani's story as part of their recitation grade. Her words, memorized by all her friends!

Viviani walked through the quiet hallways of her school, into the office. Schools were downright creepy when the heartbeat of kids was missing. Miss Hutch was there, waiting for her. Viviani proudly handed her the ditto stencil.

Miss Hutch smiled and pointed to Viviani's still-smudged cheek. "Looks like you wrestled with this assignment a bit."

Viviani laughed.

Miss Hutch squeegeed a squirt of solvent onto the drum of the ditto machine. It smelled earthy and bookish—important, like permanence should. She lodged the stencil atop the drum and pointed at the handle.

"Turn that, and your copies will come out over here," she said, motioning to a wire tray beneath the machine.

Viviani turned the metal handle with both hands. *Whoosh, whoosh, whoosh* sang the machine, and Viviani could tell why it was called a drum—the rhythm of printing was steady and solid. The smell of solvent filled the air, filled Viviani's lungs. She breathed deeply, and the scent was like inhaling stories.

Viviani's arms burned, but she wound the lever eighteen times, enough for each person in her class to get a copy of her story.

"There we go, Viviani," Miss Hutch shouted over the din, and Viviani pulled back on the lever to stop the drum from spinning out an additional copy. When the drum came to a halt, silence filled the room, and Viviani realized she missed the *whoosh whoosh whoosh*, missed the smell of words coming to life.

But ah! *Her story!* Viviani looked at the stack of papers lying in the tray. "I'm published!" she whispered. And soon, this story would be in the *Times*, too!

Miss Hutch smiled. "It's an excellent story, Viviani. Let's go share your words with your friends."

Viviani's classmates trickled into the classroom, and after teasing her for all those ink smudges ("She's like the tattooed lady at Barnum's circus!" Tommy Lutsinger said with a chortle), they all took their seats.

Miss Hutch handed the stack of papers to Jake Joseph. "Take one and pass it along, please."

She moved to the front of the class, straightening the items on her desk and beaming at Viviani. "As you know, I selected Viviani's story as the winner of our essay contest about friendship. I just loved your story, Viviani. It sounded so fresh, and yet so familiar."

Jake Joseph looked up from the piece of paper he held, his face twisted into a deep frown. "It should sound familiar. This is just like that picture book *Millions of Cats*!"

"Yeah," said Tommy Lutsinger. "My mama used to read that book to me. It does sound a lot like it."

"'Millions and billions and trillions,'" mumbled Laurel Rudolph quietly.

"You stole this, Viviani!" said Jake, his frown now a full-on scowl. "You copied *Millions of Cats*!"

Miss Hutch turned to Viviani, her face no longer beaming. "Is this true, Viviani? Did you plagiarize?"

Viviani shook her head, the classroom growing instantly hot and blurry. "It's not a copy, I swear. I just . . . I looked at *Millions of Cats* for inspiration."

"You mean you stole it," Jake Joseph said.

"It's very different," Merit said, scanning Viviani's words. "Well, kind of different." Her brow furrowed.

Oddly, Viviani noticed, Eva said nothing. She tried to catch her friend's eye, but Eva stared resolutely down at her printed copy.

Viviani's heart sank.

"Plagiarism is a very serious offense, Viviani." Miss Hutch's voice sounded like a handful of gravel shaken in a tin can. "I'll, well . . . I'll need to reread your story alongside *Millions of Cats* this weekend and compare the two. And of course, I'll need to review all of this with Mr. Criscone."

"OooOOOOoooh!" the class burbled. Mr. Criscone was the principal. This must be really, tremendously serious. Viviani sank in her seat almost as quickly as her heart sank into her stomach.

"After this weekend, I'll let you know if you're still the winner of our contest, Miss Fedeler." Viviani had never seen her beloved teacher look so stern. Or disappointed.

Now she was *Miss Fedeler*. Viviani nodded, eked out a meager "Yes, ma'am." Her face burned red and her eyes watered and her nose stung and her throat closed up and all she wanted to do was run home and bury herself under the quilts on her bed.

Had she plagiarized her story? Had she stolen the idea?

Viviani buried her face in her ink-stained hands.

Was being a story collector the same as being a story hoarder?

Viviani had never looked forward to recess as much as she did today. She dashed out to the playground to catch up with Merit and Eva, panting for breath when she finally did.

"Hey! Why didn't you wait for me?" she breathed. "I really need to—"

But Eva spun toward Viviani, eyes glittering. "It's me in the story, isn't it, Viviani?" she said, her arms crossed tight. "I'm the gentle girl you wrote about, aren't I? The timid one in your story?"

Viviani blinked. "Well, I—"

But Eva plowed ahead, voice wavering. She pulled a piece of paper from her jacket pocket. It was Viviani's story, crumpled and tearstained. "This opening line, right here: *Once upon a time there was a very gentle girl and a very gutsy girl. They lived in New York City, where the lights glittered all night. But the gentle girl was still afraid. She was afraid of the dark.*"

Eva took a wavering breath. "Everyone knows I'm your best friend, Viviani. Everyone knows that's me!"

Viviani shook her head slightly, confused. She had thought Eva would like joining her in this tale. Why wouldn't someone want to be a part of a story? An *award-winning* story? That part, she guessed, was still being decided. Her stomach churned. "Well, I was maybe inspired by you, but—"

Eva guffawed. "I can't believe you, Viviani! Do you know how embarrassing it is to have everyone know I'm still afraid of the dark? *In fifth grade?*" She looked over her shoulder, making sure no one else could hear.

Merit's eyes bounced between Viviani and Eva. "Is this true, Viv?"

Viviani was feeling really hot now. This day couldn't get any more sour! First she was accused of plagiarism, and now this?

"I didn't put your name in it," Viviani said. Now she crossed her arms, too. "No one knows that's you, Eva. Merit didn't. Right, Merit?"

Viviani thought she was going to back her up, but instead Merit shook her head and said, "That's not right, Viviani. You should've asked Eva if you could write her into your story."

"Eva is *always* written into my stories!" Viviani said, her voice growing louder, but she quieted as a group of boys approached.

"Well, lookee here," Jake Joseph snarled into their tangled-up trio. "What a pair you two make: a cheater and a scaredy-cat. Merit, you might want to pick some new friends."

He and the other boys laughed and sauntered away.

Merit glared at their backs, then reached out and twined her fingers around Eva's.

"Just think about this from Eva's side, Viviani, and how it might make you feel," Merit said gently. "You are really great at writing from someone else's perspective, after all."

The Moppets were mopey the rest of the school day, and when the bell rang and Eva and Merit walked home together without saying goodbye to Viviani, she didn't think her spirits could be dampened any more. Miss Hutch was deciding whether she had plagiarized. She wouldn't find out until Monday what her teacher—and her *principal*—thought of it all. And whether she'd be called in to meet with Mr. Criscone. And oh! If she lost the essay contest, she'd lose her story collector status! Her family would be so disappointed in her. And now, on top of *all that*, she'd been told she wasn't a good friend. What if this was the end of the Moppets?

Viviani sat on the curb, gulping air so she wouldn't cry there in front of the school, with all her classmates passing her by.

What a long, long weekend this would be.

CHAPTER TWENTY-FOUR

Book Conservation and Restoration,
Dewey Decimal 025.8

SEE ALSO: *book collecting, rare books*

T he phrase *let someone down* is such a funny twist of words.
It sounds so gentle, so loving, doesn't it, Dear Friend?
When, in actuality, letting someone down feels like disappointment so crushing, it would be better represented by
the sound of a beetle being squashed underfoot.

Viviani could *not* go home and face her parents.
Could *not* let them down. They had been so proud of
her! Viviani's insides twisted. How Papa's eyes had
glittered as he tapped the empty spot on the shelf, the
spot where her book would be placed!

Instead, she ambled around the library and found
herself entering room 100, where the picture collection resided. The last time she had been there, Eva and
Merit were with her, looking at ideas for Merit's essay.

She wondered whether the Moppets would ever be all together in this room again.

Viviani stopped short when she entered because there, hunched over a bin of photographs with Mrs. Coe: Lorena Hickok from the *New York Times*!

"What's she doing here?" Viviani whispered to herself, shrinking against a wall.

It quickly became apparent: Miss Hickok was asking for medical photos.

Medical photos!

". . . and do you happen to have a photograph of lungs?" Miss Hickok asked.

"Lungs?" Mrs. Coe replied, eyebrows knit. "We have a photo of a dissected frog's lungs, and an iron lung . . ." Mrs. Coe flipped through the bins rapidly.

Miss Hickok cracked her knuckles. "No. No, I really need a photo of *human lungs*."

Why in the *world* would this reporter want a photo of lungs? Unless she was possibly hoarding *all sorts* of medical materials! Could this *Times* reporter be the story hoarder?

Possibly.

And to Viviani, *possibly* usually meant *probably*.

Viviani was confused and sad and angry, and she knew for sure she couldn't face Mama while she was feeling so swirly-upset. So she moped around the halls of the library some more, down a flight of stairs and through the door of the Printing Office.

"Well, hello there, Viviani!" Mr. Tuttle said, looking up from his project. Old books were scattered all around him. He dabbed a bit of something—glue?—onto the rotting spine of a book. "Are you here to see your friends?"

Viviani grinned at Mr. Tuttle referring to the stack of old books as *friends*.

He grinned back. "Would you like to help me repair this old fella?"

Viviani nodded. She edged around the counter and watched as he expertly drew a thin line of yellowy glue down the seam of the leather.

"Now," he said, folding the flap of the spine around the book, "hold this tight, *right here*, please. Perfect. I'll get the clamps."

Viviani gripped the smooth, cool leather of the book. She saw its title, *Leaves of Grass*, by Walt Whitman. "One of Papa's favorites," she said.

Mr. Tuttle nodded, his neck wobbling a bit as he did. "He's not alone. This book has been well loved." He slid a small iron clamp around the top of the book and wound it tight—"not *too* tight, see, or it'll crush the cover"—around the book. He placed another clamp around the bottom half of the book.

"Now, when that dries, we'll remove the clamps and hand-stitch anything else that's loose," Mr. Tuttle said. "This one's just about ready." He picked up a different book, one with a red leather cover, and unwound the clamps that bound it.

"Light reading," Viviani said when she saw the title, *The Philosophy of Death*.

Mr. Tuttle chuckled. "Ah, but necessary, no?" He picked up a small pair of scissors, like nail cutters. "Now, turn to page three please, Viviani."

She did, and Mr. Tuttle handed her the scissors. "If you will, please nick the top right corner of the page with a V."

"Do you think I'm a sap?" Viviani asked with shocked laughter. "Cut a page of a book? Those librarians will hunt me down and lock me in their book dungeon!"

Mr. Tuttle chortled. "Ah, but, Viviani! Every book I fix gets nicked. Always on page three. It's how we note that a book not only belongs to the library but also needs to be pulled from the stacks soon. I nick the pages to let the librarians know that it's already been repaired once."

Viviani brightened. "So it's a code!"

Mr. Tuttle chuckled. "Well, yes, I suppose so. It's a code to let the librarians know that this book is close to retirement."

Viviani inhaled deeply and nodded, readying the

scissors. She looked up at Mr. Tuttle one last time. He smiled.

"It's okay, Viviani. I promise."

She snipped the page—*cha-chink!*—and the clippers left a perfect, tiny V in the top right corner of page three. A code.

Viviani exhaled. "Phew. Your job is stressful, Mr. T."

Suddenly, Merit and Eva bounded out of the dark-room down the hall. They stopped in their tracks when they saw Viviani.

Oh. *Ohhhh. That's* what Mr. Tuttle had meant when he asked if Viviani was here to see her friends. They must've come into the building off Forty-Second Street, near the children's room. Her heart felt as if it were playing the low, moany tune of a jazz saxophone.

Mr. Tuttle must've felt the tension lying thick and heavy over them like a wet wool blanket. "Did you get the pictures you were hoping for, girls?"

Merit nodded slightly. "They're grainy and dark, but we got about twelve photos of people coming and going from the Rare Books Room."

"The contraption worked!" Viviani cried. She rushed over to see the photographs, then hesitated. Was Eva still upset with her?

Viviani's skin itched; she wanted so badly to see those photos. Merit must've been able to tell, because she smiled hesitantly and said, "We were just headed up to share these with Mr. Bergquist. Want to come with us, Viviani?" Eva shifted but said nothing.

Viviani's sad heart-tune kicked up a hopeful notch. "Would I! Let's go."

The Moppets climbed the stairs to the second floor and the library investigator's office (Viviani noticed no one had to yell "Slow down, Viviani!" this time). Eva hung back a bit, but Viviani was sure she would be able to smooth things over once they got the chance to talk.

But by the time they reached G. William Bergquist's office, Viviani was about to burst. They had *photos*! Of the story hoarder! She pushed through the door ahead of her friends. (Friends? Well, after this, they surely would be again!)

"We got them," Viviani panted.

Miss Schneider stood, blinked. "Got what?"

"Photos. Of the story hoarder."

"Well, we don't know that for sure," Merit said. She dropped the stack of slick, grainy black-and-white photos onto Miss Schneider's desk. Miss Schneider picked them up, studied them one by one.

Mr. Bergquist opened the door to his office. "Miss Schneider, I need— Oh, hello, girls!"

"We captured our book borrower on camera!" Viviani nodded, pointing at the stack of photographs Miss Schneider held.

"You what?" Mr. Bergquist leaned over his assistant's shoulder. "What are these?"

"Photographs of people coming and going from the Rare Books Room," Viviani said. Her breathing had finally returned to normal, but she got excited all over again. "Twelve of them. I think the story hoarder is likely in that stack, don't you, sir?"

Mr. Bergquist flipped through the photos. Viviani felt Merit and Eva slide their eyes at each other as he studied them.

He sighed. "Girls, I'm afraid there's just no way to tell from photographs if any of these is our guy. Thank you for this effort, but these photos are just of our regular patrons, I believe. So, relatively useless for this case."

He dropped the photos on Miss Schneider's desk and paused.

"And, girls, listen." Mr. Bergquist sighed again. "I like ingenuity and inventiveness as much as anyone. But this?" He gestured to the photos he'd just tossed aside. "This is just plain meddling. I know you want to help, but you're getting in the way of this investigation. Our guy—the *story hoarder*, you called him? I like that. Anyways, this story hoarder spots something like this, rigged up in public for everyone to see, and he just stops coming around. And when that happens, we lose him."

"Lose him?" Eva asked. She gulped.

Mr. Bergquist *tsk*ed, nodded. "Yep. And if that happens, we never catch the bad guy. So, girls? *Stop meddling!*"

He picked up a file, turned, and went into his office, closing the door a little too forcefully, if you asked Viviani.

Viviani's spirits fell once again. Miss Schneider must've somehow heard them crash, seen them drop, because she laid a gentle hand on Viviani's arm. "Thank you, girls. Can we keep these photos as possible evidence? I'll add them to the file."

Possible evidence had a far nicer ring to it than *relatively useless*. Viviani nodded. Merit and Eva had already turned to leave, together. They hadn't waited for Viviani to come along.

Viviani set her jaw. She had been told she had plagiarized. She had been told she was a bad friend. And now she was being told to stop meddling. The library was her *home*. She couldn't just step aside.

"Sure you can keep those, Miss S," she said. "But don't you worry. We'll get you the evidence you need to catch this person. *Without* meddling. You mark my words!"

CHAPTER TWENTY-FIVE

Theater,

Dewey Decimal 792

SEE ALSO: *musical theater, actors and acting*

Viviani was determined to tell Mama and Papa about the pickle she was in with her essay, but when Viviani got back to the apartment, Mama was waiting with a surprise. She'd bought tickets for the whole family to see the *Ziegfeld Follies* at the New Amsterdam Theatre.

"Let's celebrate your essay, Vivi!" Mama said, and wrapped Viviani in the biggest hug. Viviani felt seasick, minus the sea. *Ugh!* She couldn't tell them about her essay now.

So Viviani got dolled up in her smart velour polka-dot dress and walked west with the rest of the family, toward the bright lights of Broadway. Her feet dragged like bricks.

"I can't wait to see the Ziegfeld Girls!" John Jr. said. He looked a little too dreamy-eyed at the prospect of seeing all those costumed ladies, so Viviani frogged him in the arm. "Which one is the standout this year, Mama?"

"Marion Davies is the one to watch, I hear," Mama said. She paused for traffic, then waved them across Sixth Avenue. Mama always knew which performers and musicians would hit the big time. She had an ear for music like no one else. "I'm really looking forward to hearing the Brox Sisters myself. Those voices! I could listen to their Tennessee accents all day."

"I can't wait to see Eddie Cantor," Papa said. "That fella is the real McCoy."

"Frances Upton is marvelous, too," Mama added. "She's the funny one in that duo, if you ask me."

The Fedeler family's excitement was contagious, and Viviani felt her steps get peppier. She began to leave her worries behind, back at the corner of Fifth and Forty-Second. She was headed toward a vaudeville spectacle—no, *the* vaudeville spectacle—and was about to see singers and showgirls and comedians and all sorts of fun and frivolous things.

The New Amsterdam Theatre was the largest, most opulent theater on Broadway. The family entered through the arched doorway, under hundreds of electrical bulbs lined up and shining like an army of light. In the lobby, Mama removed her light coat and her cloche hat and twirled her pin-curled hair back into place along her cheekbone. Papa checked the coats while Viviani took in the lobby: reliefs of characters from Shakespeare and the dramatic operas in Wagner's *Ring* cycle.

When Papa returned to join them, he bowed deeply to a gold carving of Hamlet clutching a skull and recited:

"Doubt thou the stars are fire;
Doubt that the sun doth move;
Doubt truth to be a liar;
But never doubt I love."

Papa swept up and grabbed Mama about the waist. He twirled, spun, and dipped her, and Viviani's heart swelled as she watched her parents dance. Mama was powdered and perfumed and pearled. Papa was slicked and sharp and spiffy. They were quite the lookers.

"Cut it out, you two!" Edouard mumbled. He cut his eyes to both sides, no doubt making sure no one he knew was there. "Fact: you are very embarrassing."

The Fedelers took one of the gilded elevators up to their seats. The theater itself looked as though it had been carved inside a giant redwood tree, but brightly painted. The carvings depicting Aesop's fables were Viviani's favorites.

"*Psst*," John Jr. whispered to Viv after they'd taken

their seats. "You know this theater is haunted, right? Showgirl named Olive, died by mercury poisoning."

Viviani whacked John Jr. with her *Playbill*. "Is not."

Edouard leaned around him. "*That* is a fact."

Viviani stuck her tongue out at her brothers. Always trying to scare her! But hadn't she heard something about a ghost who blew kisses to an audience? Viviani shivered. (Lightly, not giving her brothers the satisfaction of seeing her get the willies.)

The lights lowered; the crowd hushed. The show began with a breathtaking burst of feathers and sequins and light!

Viviani felt herself get floatier. Despite all her worries, the earth was still spinning light to dark and back again, and New York City was alive with art.

And then the comedy duo Papa had been waiting for arrived: Eddie Cantor and Frances Upton, entering in a whoosh of pratfalls while trombones slid *whannnah-whaannnn* to accentuate their trips and stunts.

Viviani snuck a glance at Papa's wide smile in the dim blue light. Papa's smile always make Viviani feel warm and safe, like everything would be okay as long as that grin was in place.

After their big entrance, Eddie elbowed Frances. "Hey, Frances. You're a great pal, you know that?"

"Well, friends are the people who know you really well and like you anyway."

The drummer hit a rimshot, *ba-DUM! Chhh!*

"Yeah, Eddie. We've been friends so long I can't remember which one of us is the bad influence."

The audience chuckled, nodded. John Jr. elbowed Edouard. Viviani blinked.

Friendship? This skit was about *friendship*? Her essay on this very subject was now under scrutiny. And Viviani wasn't certain she still *had* any friends! Her shoulders drooped, and she could practically hear the trombone slide accentuating the drop: *whannnahwhaannnn.*

"Eddie, tell me three things about yourself, friend."

Eddie held up a single finger. "Well, number one. I'm lazy." He stopped. Shrugged. There was no two or three. Laughter from the audience filled the theater. The row of Fedelers chuckled.

"Yeah, but I'm getting older, Frances. I can tell because I have more candles on my birthday cake than friends at my party."

More laughter. More Fedeler fun. But Viviani sank slightly into her seat. Would Merit or Eva still come to *her* party?

"A true friend is someone who thinks you're a good egg even though you're slightly cracked."

The audience roared. Mama swiped at the corners of her eyes with the back of her hand, she was laughing so hard. Edouard slapped his knee. Everyone was having a grand time. Everyone except Viviani.

The rest of the show was outstanding—music and laughter and sets and costumes and makeup. But oh! How Viviani's heart hurt for her bruised friendships, for her battered words. Viviani's feet dragged the whole two-and-a-half-block walk home, and she didn't even stay in the living room while John Jr. and Edouard reenacted the scenes.

Viviani needed to turn *her* story around.

CHAPTER TWENTY-SIX

Journalism—Objectivity,

Dewey Decimal 302.23

SEE ALSO: *mass media—objectivity; journalism—political aspects*

F or all of Saturday and some of Sunday, Viviani absentmindedly wandered the library halls, trying to keep her
mind off the fact that tomorrow she could be meeting with
the school principal. She spotted Papa carrying a ladder
ahead and scurried to catch up with him. "Hey, Papa! You
maybe, uh, need a hand today? How about I work with you
and you tell me a story or two?" Viviani could use a little
familiarity in her routine and a whole lot of distraction.

Papa chucked her on the chin. "I'd love to, Firecracker, but I can't. Lots of crawl-space work today, and
that's a job built for one. Hey, why don't you go write
down one of your famous stories yourself? I'll read it
later!"

Off Papa went, without even knowing he'd torn out Viviani's heart and stomped on it.

Just then, pushing through the revolving front doors like a hurricane, came that woman reporter, Lorena Hickok, from the *New York Times*!

"Zowie," Viviani whispered, her mood brightening. Here was a double opportunity: follow her to see whether she was checking out more books *and* see what kinds of stories she was working on for the *Times*. It was awfully odd that several of the books she requested were on the "missing" list. It was worth more investigation.

That wasn't meddling, was it? Not the kind of thing Mr. Bergquist meant? No, Viviani would simply . . . follow her up the stairs . . . and around the corner . . . and up another flight . . . and oh! What a coincidence! Viviani was *also* going into the Main Reading Room! And OOOOH! Viviani's heart galloped when she saw where Miss Hickok was headed: the Rare Books Room.

Bingo!

Viviani ducked into a chair at one of the hundreds of tables and picked up a book already there: *Mating Habits of the Sperm Whale*. She opened it, then peered around its edge at Miss Hickok.

The journalist knocked, and Miss Fillipelli unlocked the door. "Credentials, please?" Miss Fillipelli said loudly.

"I'm sorry?" Miss Hickok asked. "You know I'm with the *Times*."

"An ID," Miss Fillipelli replied. "I need to see some identification."

"You've never needed to see it before," Miss Hickok said.

"Never had several thousand dollars' worth of books gone missing before," Miss Fillipelli said firmly, crossing her arms.

Miss Hickok sighed, but she dug around in a pouch and brought out a large yellow slip of paper. Her driver's license.

Miss Fillipelli unfolded it, read it, and looked up at Miss Hickok as though she were peering over glasses. "Come on in, Miss Hickok."

If Miss Fillipelli was so suspicious, there *must* be something untrustworthy about the journalist! Viviani waited until the door clicked closed behind what was likely the story hoarder. Then she leapt to her feet, sprang forward, and knocked on the door.

Miss Fillipelli opened it. She scowled when she saw it was Viviani, and Viv realized they hadn't seen each other since Viviani had trapped her with the Rube Goldberg invention. She blazed red.

"No," Miss Fillipelli said, head shaking furiously. "No entry, Miss Fedeler. Strict rules from Dr. Anderson:

no one visits the Rare Books Room without credentials. Not until we locate those overdue books."

"But—" Viviani began, and the door closed in her face. Viviani imagined it would've slammed had it not been designed to close quietly.

"—our hoarder might be in there," Viviani whispered. She touched the leather-covered door lightly.

CHAPTER TWENTY-SEVEN

Idea (Philosophy),
Dewey Decimal 158.1

SEE ALSO: *affirmations, self-confidence (miscellaneous)*

Viviani waited in the Main Reading Room until Miss Hickok left, then tailed her out, catching bits of her grumbling, "Missing! All the books I need for this piece—checked out! Overdue! How am I going to break this story?"

Viviani paused and second-guessed Miss Hickok as a suspect. Why would Miss Hickok bother requesting them *after* checking them out? To cover her tracks, maybe?

And for a reporter, Miss Hickok certainly wasn't very observant; she never noticed Viviani creeping along behind her, not even when she pushed through the revolving front door right on her heels. Viviani stopped at the top of the stairs and watched her mumble away.

Viviani's emotions had felt whirled on the wind lately, and this encounter was no different. She couldn't figure out what to make of this woman and her intense gaze. On one hand, she wrote for the *New York Times*, one of the most respected newspapers in the world. She seemed very committed to her story, which Viviani certainly understood. On the other hand, she seemed to understand something about the pattern of overdue books that Viviani hadn't seen.

Viviani sighed and made her way back inside to the apartment; she couldn't follow Miss Hickok throughout the city. Well, she *could*, but Mama was still irked about the whole contraption business, and Viviani didn't want to push her. When she opened the front door, Mama smiled and looked up from her book. "Hey, there's a juggling competition going on in Bryant Park. Want to go?"

Viviani shook her head. "No, thanks." She sulked to her room, sank into her soft bed. Sure enough, outside her window in the park below, she could see folks juggling multiple colored balls. Bowling pins. Even flames and knives.

Boy, did she know what that felt like! All those things up in the air, the panic of watching them all fall, trying to catch them . . .

Mama rapped softly on the door, creaked it open. "Everything okay, Viv?"

Viviani flopped backward onto her bed. She couldn't stop the tears that stung her eyes. *Nothing* was okay, but she didn't know how to begin spelling it all out for her mother. She hadn't told her parents about Eva being mad at her. She hadn't told her parents that Mr. Bergquist was frustrated with her. And she most certainly hadn't told her parents about the fact that maybe—*maybe*—she'd stolen her story and hadn't won the essay contest after all.

"Mama, this story hoarder is terrible," she said. What she meant was, *I might've plagiarized a story and I feel terrible.*

"Oh, yes, I totally agree," Mama said, and then she muttered in Spanish under her breath. Mama did that when she was truly angry and didn't want her kids to know she was cursing. What she *didn't* know was that the Fedeler kids had long ago figured out what those words meant. Thank you, library!

Viviani blinked. "I thought you'd say something like, *Viviani, we have to be forgiving.* Or *Viviani, he wasn't born terrible.*"

"Why should I? You already know that," Mama said with a wink. "No, this person angers me, too. He's not just hoarding *things*, Viv. He's hoarding *ideas*." Mama ran her fingers through Viviani's curls. It had been a while since she'd done that, and Viviani sighed and closed her eyes.

"Things can be replaced. Ideas can't. And this fellow is being very stingy with some very big ideas."

Viviani sank deeper into her pillow. "This isn't making me feel better." She didn't go into exactly *why*. It was right there on the tip of her tongue—*Mama, they think I stole that story I wrote*—and yet she didn't say it. Couldn't. Her family was just too proud of her.

"Maybe you could write in your captain's log," Mama said gently.

"What's the point?" Viviani frowned. What if she ended up accidentally plagiarizing another idea?

"Viviani, I'm upset, too," Mama said, stroking Viviani's curls. "That's the whole reason libraries exist, after all: to share ideas. So we just have to keep sharing as many ideas as possible. As widely as possible. With as many people as possible. We can't let one selfish person take that away."

Viviani imagined these ideas as butterflies, turned loose across a bright blue sky. They'd flit and flop and flip and collide, and soon they'd find the stream of air they needed to drift, until they found the exact right flower to call home.

"Thanks, Mama," Viviani said.

Mama gave her a sloppy wet kiss in the center of her forehead. "Now, get out that captain's log of yours and start sharing your ideas, kiddo."

Outside and below, a juggler tossing fire dropped a lit baton. It fizzled out in the wet grass, turning to smoke.

But he scooped it up and quickly lit it, using another of his fiery batons.

Viviani watched as the original fire became two fires, both equally big and strong. Nothing disappeared from the first fire to make the second; it wasn't lessened in any way.

That's how stories and ideas work, Viviani thought. *You share them, they ignite, and they grow.*

That's what she'd always wanted to do with words. She'd never meant to steal or sneak. She'd only wanted to share words, ignite others, and watch her ideas grow.

Dear Friend,

> *Did I do it?*
>
> *Did I steal that story idea?*
>
> *I keep wondering about ideas, and whether it's TRULY possible to steal them. Stealing an idea is like cheating love, or borrowing hate, or lending joy. Those things aren't possible, are they?*
>
> *Yeah, they are.*
>
> *They are, and I know it.*
>
> *It makes me think about our story hoarder and those books. The books he's holding on to*

are so rare that they are probably the only place in the world where THOSE particular ideas exist. Hoarding those books IS being greedy with those ideas.

Was I so greedy to prove myself a true writer that I used someone else's idea?

Eva's mad at me, too. Did I steal HER story? Oh, I didn't mean to—not at all, never! She's just so much more interesting than most people I know. Funny and brave but never a show-off. To me, most people seem to be painted like a straight line, all one color, unbreaking and unbending. Not Eva. She's swirly and swoopy and colorful, and I never know what to expect. That's why she's my best friend.

I just hope John Jr. and Edouard don't hear about all this at school. Oh, I don't want to disappoint my family, too!

I never TOOK anything. <u>Millions of Cats</u> is still on its shelf in the children's room, making kids (and Mr. Green) smile. At what point does inspiration become stealing?

Today's code is fairly simple, Friend. It replaces symbols with letters:

a = ♋

d = ♎

e = ♏

h = ≋

i = ♓

l = ●

o = □

r = □

s = ♦

t = ◆

y = ⬒

? = ✐

♎♓♎　♓　♎□　♓♦✐

♎♓♎　♓　♦◆♏♋●　◆≋♋◆

♦◆□□⬒　♓♎♏♋✐

CHAPTER TWENTY-EIGHT

Underwater Exploration,
Dewey Decimal 551

SEE ALSO: *underground areas, earth (planet)*

Things More Terrible Than Being Accused
of Plagiarism:

–getting mauled by a tiger (I imagine)

–the plague

–book burning

–That's it. That's all I got. Not even going
to the doctor is worse.

Monday morning in the schoolyard, Viviani arrived, feet dragging, eyelids drooping. What a terrible night's sleep she'd had. Toss! Turn! Flop! Flip! A guilty conscience makes for a restless night.

She should've let Eva know that *she* was as much an inspiration for her story as *Millions of Cats*.

She should've let Mama know that she was going to the principal's office today.

But was she guilty of stealing that story?

The bell rang, and students began to file inside. Miss Hutch stood just inside the door.

"Viviani, please follow me to Mr. Criscone's office."

"OoooooOOOOOOH," Viviani's classmates chorused.

"She's gonna get it now!" Jake Joseph whispered loudly.

"Bet she gets paddled. Just watch."

"She should! She stole that story."

Then, above the others, Viviani heard Eva, her voice sharp as knives: "No, she didn't! She used that story for inspiration! There's a difference!"

Merit's voice lifted up next: "Viviani Fedeler is many things, but she is not a thief."

The Moppets still supported her! Even when they were mad at her. It made her lift her chin against the impending doom. Viviani gave them a small smile.

"Still," someone else chimed in. It sounded like Jake Joseph again. "She deserves to see the principal."

Viviani gulped. The principal's office!

She'd never been inside Mr. Criscone's office. Sure, she'd heard stories—mostly from John Jr. She expected sharp instruments of torture and cold steel walls, from what she'd heard. She shuddered. Her chest tightened.

The hallway to the principal's office was three hundred miles long, or so it seemed this morning. Viviani grew thirsty, imagining herself plodding forty years through a hot desert.

The school secretary, Mrs. Ahmed, smiled. "Good morning!" she chirruped.

Viviani thought of her as the canary in the coal mine, the beautiful bird that sings when there's a dangerous gas leak: *"Get out! Get out!"*

The door to Mr. Criscone's office *creeeeeeep*ed open. Miss Hutch flipped the lightbulb switch. Oh!

The room was wood-paneled, dark like a cave. But most outstanding were the dozens of fish tanks!

There were small clear globes, each containing a single flowy fish. There were huge globes on intricate iron stands—like the globes of earth in the library's map room, but these were glass—containing maybe ten or twelve bright orange fish each. And then there was a single huge tank, the legs of which were sculpted iron seahorses! That tank had rocks and plants and little figures on the bottom: a sunken pirate ship, an open treasure chest. That aquarium must've held thirty fish—blue, orange, yellow, zebra-striped—and they painted waves with their swishy colorful fins.

Any other time, Viviani would've been positively charmed by the rainbows of color and the soft, watery glow the tanks emitted. But today? Today, she found all this water suffocating, like she was trying to see how long she could hold her breath. She gulped air.

"Have a seat, Viviani," Miss Hutch said, pointing to one of the stern wooden chairs facing Mr. Criscone's desk. She peered at it before sitting. It didn't appear to have any locking mechanisms that could constrain her while they extracted the truth from her with poky things.

Miss Hutch sat in the other small chair. "Mr. Criscone will be—"

At that moment, Mr. Criscone whirled in like a tornado of papers and file folders. His shiny bald head gleamed as he took a seat opposite Viviani.

Her palms began sweating.

Mr. Criscone peered at Viviani over his tiny wire-rimmed spectacles. Nearby, one of the fish tanks burbled. It matched the sound of Viviani's stomach.

"Let's see now," he began. "Ahem. We must address this use of stink bombs in the toilets, Miss—"

Miss Hutch cleared her throat. "Excuse me, Mr. Criscone. This is Viviani. Fedeler? The winner of the essay contest."

Mr. Criscone nodded emphatically. "Ah, yes, yes." He shuffled some papers around. The fish tanks blooped and plipped. Viviani hoped she could hold her breakfast down.

"Viviani, Viviani . . . ," he droned, looking at each piece of paper. "Accused of plagiarism, yes?"

Accused. Viviani's pulse pounded so loud, she could barely hear him. If she'd truly stolen that story, would she *only* get paddled? Maybe her punishment would be worse! Maybe she'd go to *jail*!

Viviani's chest tightened further. How long could she stay underwater?

"Ah, yes, here it is." Mr. Criscone found the file he was looking for. Viviani's ears rang. She blinked. Would they lead her out of the school in handcuffs? Oh, if her picture was in the papers wearing black-and-white stripes, she'd have a list of chores so long, she'd need the librarians to catalog them.

"Yes, well. After reading both stories, Miss Hutch and I have determined that your story, Viviani, is—"

Viviani watched Mr. Criscone's mouth silently form the last part, because between her ringing ears and her held breath and those plooping fish tanks, she could no longer hear:

"—is inspired by the original, but it is *not* plagiarized.

The room fell silent. Viviani turned to Miss Hutch. "What?"

Miss Hutch smiled. "Your story is original, Viviani. Not a copy. Granted, there is a fine line. But ultimately, we decided that your story was different enough from the original to be considered unique. Congratulations, Viviani. You are the winner of the essay contest. Fair and square."

Viviani was so thrilled that she didn't even point out Edouard's fact that the phrase meant "fair and fair." She squealed, leapt to her feet. Suddenly, the room seemed bursting with color and light and magical flowy suspended fish. She hugged Miss Hutch, then danced around the desk and hugged Mr. Criscone, too. She hugged the principal!

"*Thank you, thank you!*" she sang.

Mr. Criscone chuckled awkwardly. "Ahem. Yes. Now get to class." He turned to Miss Hutch. "Miss Hutch, I need to speak with you this afternoon. We might need to combine Miss King's class with yours. It'll be tight, and a lot of extra work. But she's going to be out for a while with"—his voice fell to a whisper—"tuberculosis."

Viviani's stomach plummeted. Miss King, sick? She'd been Viviani's teacher last year. She was so young, and she lived in the city all by herself, in a boardinghouse. She always talked about the adventures she and her boardinghouse friends went on together—she told the class she'd cried when they visited the Statue of Liberty for the first time. Were they all sick?

Miss Hutch placed her fingertips over her lips. "Certainly. Whatever help I can give. Is she okay?"

Mr. Criscone had already shifted to a different stack of papers. "I suppose so. Her parents live upstate, so she's able to treat herself to some fresh air. Living on top of each other in this city can really wreak havoc."

Viviani and Miss Hutch left the office. The hallway had shrunken back to its original length and was now only several hundred feet long. As Viviani and Miss Hutch approached the stairs, the teacher gently touched Viviani's elbow.

"I'm delighted this worked out, Viviani. But next time, you really need to be cautious in choosing what inspires you, and you should always name your sources."

"Yes, ma'am."

"You have plenty of stories of friendship, from what I've seen." Miss Hutch smiled warmly. Viviani thought of the Moppets and how they had stood by her side, even when they were angry at her. That's what true friends did.

"Miss Hutch? Do you think Eva and Merit could come with me to the *Times* headquarters? The essay was about friendship, after all, and, well, we're kinda a trilogy."

Miss Hutch laughed. "I think that's a marvelous idea, Viviani."

Viviani couldn't wait to tell the Moppets. Eva had wanted to see the huge printing presses churning out the news, and Merit would get to see all those photographs and photographers and darkrooms and cameras! And Viviani? Her story would appear in the pages of the *New York Times*! She'd be a published author! In print! With readers! It's what her heart had always wanted: she'd share her words, ignite others, and watch ideas grow.

Viviani breathed deeply and smiled. She'd really won!

Viviani did something she'd never done before. She let Eva and Merit read what she'd written in her captain's log yesterday. Her cheeks burned the whole time they studied the page. She was dying to ask them to join her at the *Times* office, but she had to set things right first.

Please, please let her forgive me, Viviani thought.

Finally, Eva looked up. "Oh, Viv. You didn't *steal* my story. I love being included in your tall tales! But how you described me . . . is that really how you see me? Scared and weak?"

"Of course not! Just the opposite! Listen, remember when we went hunting for Big Red? At night, in the library, with only a flashlight to see by?"

Eva shuddered. "How could I forget?"

"Eva, you did that *even though you were scared*. I think that's the bravest thing a person can do. Walk straight into something even though they're frightened."

There was a pause, and Viviani gulped. "So what do you say? Want to come to the *New York Times* with me? Both of you?"

Eva glanced at Merit, who gave her a tiny smile. Eva threw her arms around Viviani's neck. "Oh, Vivi! I can't *wait* to see those printing presses! They say you can feel them drumming in your belly!"

Viviani hugged Eva back, hard. She knew all about drumming in her belly, all right. Her romping, stomping belly was finally settling down, now that she knew she was innocent. And now that the Moppets were a trio once again.

CHAPTER TWENTY-NINE

Clothing and Dress,
Dewey Decimal 646

SEE ALSO: *fashion, children's clothing*

"**C**'mon, Viviani. We're going dress shopping."

Viviani considered which combination of six words could possibly be worse than those:

"I'm pulling out your toenails now."

"Try eating this raw liver, Viviani."

"Your room is indeed haunted. 'Night!"

But Mama was standing there, leaning against the doorframe of Viviani's bedroom, arms crossed, a dishcloth dangling from one hand. Her *I mean business* stance. There was nowhere to run. Nowhere to hide.

"But I—"

"Listen. No child of mine is going into the *New York Times* headquarters wearing a faded, old, ill-fitting sack.

C'mon—it'll be fun! Merit and Eva and their parents are coming, too."

Okay, that *was* a little better.

"Why can't we just buy some sharp new clothes at Rogers Peet?" Normally an argument like this was a smart one with Mama. Eva's papa worked there, and Mama loved supporting businesses that employed their friends. But:

"Viviani. That's a men's store and you know it."

"I'd look right smart in some knickerbockers and a newsboy cap."

Mama fought a grin. "Imagine the stir we'd create, sending our girl to such an event in *pants!*"

Viviani laughed. "That *Times* reporter who's always here? Miss Hickok? She wears pants!"

Mama's eyes gleamed. She was always one for adding more pepper to the pot. "Okay—deal!"

Viviani squealed and hugged Mama's neck.

"But listen—we still have to go dress shopping. They're waiting on us now." Mama *pop*ped Viviani with a flick of the dish towel. "Move it, kiddo. You know Mr. Derian. Five minutes early is late!"

Viviani and Mama scrambled to the corner of Fifth and Forty-Second, where they met up with Merit and her mother and Eva and her dad. Eva's dad was dressed to the nines, as he was every time he left his job as super at

Rogers Peet. He sported a sharp vest, an ascot with a gold pin, a pocket watch on a chain, striped pants, and spats over his shoes. Papa always said he was the best-dressed super in town. Viviani guessed he had learned a thing or two being around all those fancy men's clothes all day.

"Now, don't you look swell," Mama said to him.

Mr. Derian tugged at the hem of his vest. "Thank you, m'lady." He bowed to her and Mrs. Mubarak. "Now—to the Garment District!"

Mr. Derian pointed a finger south, and away they marched.

"I feel like I'm being led into battle," Viviani whispered to Eva.

Eva nodded sullenly. "Might as well be." She loved clothes, adored shopping, but going with her father was quite the experience.

Mr. Derian led the herd to the heart of the district, at Thirty-Seventh Street. From this spot, you could hear the hum of huge sewing machines as they purred inside limestone and brick buildings. Bits of colorful thread and tufts of textiles floated through the air, like tiny dancing fabric fairies. Viviani sneezed, walking into this hazy rainbow.

The Garment District was special, and few people actually shopped here, Viviani knew. Most shopped at the retail stores around Fifth Avenue. But Mr. Derian had pulled a few strings (*ha!* Viviani had laughed when

Mama had said that—"pulled strings!") and was able to get an appointment directly with a clothing manufacturer, which would save them quite a bit of money.

Mr. Derian led them to a tall, skinny building and up several flights of stairs, into a narrow room that was a city block long and lined with rows and rows and rows of dresses.

Eva glowed. Viviani glowered. "I don't have to still try them *on*, do I, Mama?"

"Oh, Viv, humor me." Mama ran a finger along the hangers. "Would you look at all these glorious clothes?"

Eva and Merit began pulling dresses off hangers in a frenzy.

"This one!" Eva said, holding a fully sequined number under her chin.

"Sequins in the day?" Mr. Derian placed a fist against his heart. *"Hivand em!"*

Viviani giggled. She'd been around the Derian family enough to pick up a few Armenian phrases. Mr. Derian had said, "I am sick."

Merit spun around with a fringy sleeveless frock. "Oh, look at this one!"

Merit's mother shook her head, her black hair gleaming. "No fringe, *habibti*. And sleeves, yes?"

"But oh, look!" Eva pulled a dress from a rack that was, well, *very* short. Like, showing-one's-knees short. "What do you think, Papa?"

Viviani burst out laughing at the sight of Mr. Derian's face, which was turning bright purple.

"Shopping with your dad is fun!" Viviani said, wiping a tear from the corner of her eye.

"Yeah, sure," Eva grumbled. She dropped the short dress on a nearby chair.

At last, Merit and Eva found frocks that satisfied everyone: a sharp sailor-themed dress with a long navy tie for Eva, a dress with a very modern zigzag hemline for Merit. Viviani was excited to add a pair of pants to her wardrobe, even though Mr. Derian shook his head, mumbling, "*Chem sirum . . .*"

He shuffled off to negotiate prices.

Mama placed a deep green cloche hat on Viviani's head and tugged gently at one of her curls. "Are you ready to make your publishing debut?"

Viviani grinned. "I am! Also ready to make headlines again, related to the library. Want to hear it?"

"Absolutely."

Viviani thrust her chin in the air. "Library Moppets Crack the Code and Save the Books!"

Mama straightened the hat. "I sure like the sound of that."

"Do you bow or something when you meet the owner of the *Times*?" Eva asked on the walk home.

"Like meeting the queen?" Merit asked.

Viviani swept in front of them, bowing deeply. "So pleased to meet you, *Gray Lady*."

"Gray lady?"

Viviani nodded. "That's the paper's nickname. 'The Gray Lady.' Doesn't it sound so proper?"

Merit and Eva bowed to each other, giggling. Viviani joined in. "Hello, Gray Lady."

"Pleased to meet you, Gray Lady."

"The pleasure is all mine, Gray Lady."

The Moppets doubled over in laughter. Boy, had Viviani missed this!

CHAPTER THIRTY

Newspaper Publishing—United States,
Dewey Decimal 920

SEE ALSO: *publishers and publishing—United States*

Sometimes there's this . . . *feeling* . . . of being a part of something bigger than yourself. It's almost as though your eyes can see beyond the horizon, as though your spirit can reach beyond the confines of your skin. Perhaps you are a teammate, or a coworker, or a volunteer, or, heck, even a bee in a colony—but you are an important part of something big and buzzy and full and complete.

That's how Viviani felt, walking toward the New York Times building.

Just a few months ago, the *Times* had installed a news "zipper" on its old building in Times Square. Nearly fifteen thousand lightbulbs allowed headlines to crawl around the building like words suddenly brought to life. Viv had seen the sign flash headlines like TESLA GETS PATENTS ON HELICOPTER-PLANE and RICHARD E. BYRD STARTS EXPEDITION TO ANTARCTIC and GERMAN GRAF ZEPPELIN LZ-127 LANDS IN U.S. AFTER 93 HOURS IN FLIGHT. Now the ticker sang the newspaper's slogan, ALL THE NEWS THAT'S FIT TO PRINT. They passed by this amazing new technology as they walked through Times Square on their way to 229 West Forty-Third Street.

Viviani gasped when they arrived.

The home of the *Times* was eighteen dignified stories tall—a staid white building with a copper roof and cupola, now turned green in the sea air. THE NEW YORK TIMES was chiseled in small, precise letters above the entryway.

Click! Merit snapped a photo. Viviani smiled, squeezed Merit's elbow.

The lobby was simple and wide, and a woman with a warm smile welcomed them. "Hello, hello!" she boomed. She thrust out her hand. "Lorena Hickok. Nice threads," she said, eyeballing Viviani's new knickers and cap. Lorena, too, was wearing pants. Viviani grinned.

It was *her*! It was the woman who had been doing all that medical research in the library! Maybe they'd discover how Miss Hickok fit into all this missing-book mess today; Viviani was sure determined to figure it out.

Merit and Eva must've picked up on the fact that Miss Hickok was a suspect, too; Eva elbowed Merit, and Merit nodded.

"Put 'er there," Lorena said. Viviani put her hand in Lorena's, and her whole arm—her whole *self*—pumped up and down thanks to Miss Hickok's vigorous handshake.

"I gotta say, was I ever glad to see it was a girl who won that contest. We need more good women in this field. That we do," Lorena said, still pumping Viviani's hand like a water spigot. Her smile grew.

Viviani introduced Eva (who immediately asked, "Do you know Buster Keaton?") and Merit (who immediately said, "I take great offense to Tom Howard photographing Ruth Snyder during her electrocution, don't you?"), and of course herself ("Thank you ever so much, Miss Hickok, but I also have a lot of questions for you . . .").

Lorena interrupted Viviani and beamed at the trio. "Well, now, I don't feel I'm so far removed from you as to have earned a 'Miss.' So I want you to call me Lorena, got it?"

Viviani and friends smiled, nodded. Calling an adult by her first name! Viviani was starting to have very mixed feelings about this woman. She was so likable! But Viviani knew from experience that the "bad guy" was often very charming.

"Good," Lorena said with a single, decisive nod. "We're

gonna get along just fine now. Just fine. Let's start at the top, shall we? I'll answer as many questions as I can."

Viviani decided she'd wait until the end of the tour to question this woman's library visits. Maybe Lorena would slip up and confess something before then.

The four rode an elevator to the tenth floor. When the doors opened, the girls gasped.

"It looks like a castle!" Viviani said. The room was a library, straight out of medieval days: tall leaded-glass windows, vaulted ceilings, and thick carved oak furniture that somehow brought to Viviani's mind knights and dragons and swords and family crests.

Lorena circled the massive table. "This is where the editorial meeting happens. The editors are the ones who decide which stories get into print and, well, which ones get the ax."

Viviani ran her fingertips across the smooth tabletop. Huh—that was something she'd never thought about: all the stories that *don't* make it into print. All the stories she'd never know. It made her pluck a bit less plucky, thinking of those lost tales.

"You guys tell us what we should think about," Viviani said. "What we should worry about. What we should *know*, just by selecting which stories have value and which ones don't." But Viviani was finding there were lots of ways a story could be valuable. It was interesting to think of the different ways a story could have worth. And how what was worthy to one person might be worthless to another.

Lorena nodded. "Exactly. We direct the national conversation. Well, the *world* conversation, I suppose. Right here at this table. It's a big responsibility, one we take very seriously. There's a limited amount of paper we can afford for each news run. The stories we print take up valuable space. They must be worth every inch."

Viviani nodded. Yet another way to consider a story "valuable."

Lorena led the Moppets back onto the elevator. "Let's hit the newsroom next," she said, pushing the number three button.

"Yes!" Viviani said. Her breathing sped up up up as the elevator dinged down down down. On floor three, the doors slid open and Viviani's heart leapt out, the rest of her following behind it, scrambling to catch up.

Viviani stepped off the elevator into a perfect hurricane of ringing telephones and clacking typewriters and clanging file drawers and hustling people and muddy coffee and dirty desks and shouted stories.

The entire floor was wide open, with three long rows of wooden desks, one after another, each with a telephone, a typewriter, and a chair. The ceiling was a mess of wires and lightbulbs; the desks were a mess of paper and pens. Around the room were armies of metal file cabinets and bookshelves.

"Someone get me Amelia on the phone now!" a voice shouted. "Who has her number? Amelia Earhart?"

"I need a quote about the tunnel that the city built to Queens," someone else shouted. "Who's the best person in Mayor Walker's office to talk to?"

"Can I quote you on that?" a third person shouted into a telephone mouthpiece. "Yes, yes, of course. How do you spell your last name, Mr. Papadopoulos? And can you verify the title of your book? I want to make certain my notes are correct."

Viviani paused near this desk, listening hard. Lorena must've noticed that this conversation had drawn Viviani's attention, because she whispered, "We quote books and authors all the time as expert opinions. He's making sure he gives proper credit to his source. We often want to summarize others' ideas as part of our pieces, but we need to give them credit for inspiring us. We certainly don't want to plagiarize."

Viviani nodded emphatically—yes! *This* is what she should've done with her story "Millions of Stars" right from the get-go. If she'd noted *Millions of Cats* was the inspiration for her piece, maybe she wouldn't have gotten into her earlier sticky situation.

Viviani found Merit huddled near two people who were studying teeny-tiny prints of photographs with an eyepiece. Merit then had a turn studying the photos, and a woman in a yellow dress pointed to one of them with a pencil eraser. "We're going to use number forty-eight. Can you see why?"

Merit studied number forty-eight before bursting into laughter. "The cat! Oh, my. He's midpounce! Look at those teeth!"

"Exactly," the woman in yellow said. "You see the cat pouncing, but as a reader, you don't know for certain if he caught the mouse. The story continues outside the photograph if you don't answer every question."

Merit smiled, nodded. "Got it."

The Moppets then followed Lorena to the basement, and when the elevator doors slid open, there was no mistaking where they were:

"The printing presses!" Eva squealed, leaping forward.

The room smelled of ink and newsprint, and huge metal machines *whoosh*ed *whoosh*ed *whoosh*ed great swaths of newsprint across their massive drums. It was far larger than the ditto machine Viviani had used at school.

The blank paper spooled into one end of a press, swooshed through it like lightning, and emerged from the other side printed with millions of important words. The paper was then cut, folded, and stacked on the second half of the machine. Workers pulled stacks of paper off the runners, bound them with twine, and threw them into the back of a truck. In mere minutes, the girls watched a truck get filled with thousands of pages of newsprint—so many millions of words!—and zoom away, to a place where readers awaited the news.

"It's so fast!" Merit shouted over the noise of the presses.

Lorena nodded and shouted back, "We print over four hundred thousand copies a day! Over seven hundred fifty thousand on Sundays!"

"Wow," Viviani breathed. She had been so excited to have the eighteen kids in her class read her stories. She could barely fathom 750,000 people reading her words!

The tour was winding down, so the girls followed Lorena back up to the lobby.

"Viviani," Lorena said seriously, "We're excited to print your essay. Should run early next week. It'll be a nice change of pace from what I've been working on. Right now I'm researching a story about the ongoing tuberculosis epidemic. Been doing gobs of research at the library, but boy, am I ever stuck."

Lorena paused, and Viviani realized *this* was her moment to question the reporter about her library visits. She cracked her knuckles. Licked her lips. At the exact moment Viviani said, "So, you visit the library a lot, eh?" Lorena said, "Every book I need is missing."

Viviani jolted to attention. "What was that? What did you say?"

"Every book I need is missing. Overdue, they tell me. Every last one."

"No, no! Before that! What did you say you're researching?"

Lorena squinted at Viv. "The tuberculosis epidemic. Boy, the city thought they had this thing under control *years* ago. You know TB is the reason why spitting in public was outlawed? Except into spittoons. Wild, eh? A little gross history for you. Yeah, TB is particularly bad this—"

Viviani nearly hugged the reporter. This was huge! Another piece of the puzzle, another part of the code. Tuberculosis! The answer was *right there*, Viviani could taste it! Her feet were practically pulling her out of the Times building and back toward the library to study those titles again.

"Thank you ever so much for the tour, Lorena! Bye!" Viviani grabbed Eva's hand, then Merit's, and pulled them toward the door. Both were quite confused by this abrupt departure.

Lorena nodded distractedly, said goodbye, and stepped into the elevator to fly up to the third floor.

As the trio of Moppets galloped back toward the library, Merit and Eva looked at Viviani as if she'd grown a second head. "What was that all about, Viv?" Merit asked.

Viviani raised a single eyebrow. "I think we're looking at the missing book titles the wrong way. What Lorena said about TB? This might be *exactly* what we need to crack this case wide open!"

CHAPTER THIRTY-ONE

Tuberculosis,

Dewey Decimal 614.54

SEE ALSO: *tuberculosis—history; germ theory of disease—history*

"This was *not* what we needed to crack this case wide open." Back in Viviani's bedroom, the girls sprawled on the colorful braided-rag rug while Viviani flipped open her captain's log to a familiar page: the list of books now officially classified as "Missing/Overdue."

"I thought this might show us something," Viviani said. "Originally the librarians put the missing books in alphabetical order, because, well, they're librarians. I imagine their spice racks are alphabetized. But! When we put them in the order they went missing . . ." Viviani tapped the list with the pair of scissors she'd used to cut the list into separate scraps:

—*Health Almanac 1920*, checked out
January 16, 1929

—*Textbook of Bacteriology*, checked out
January 20, 1929

—*Anaerobic Bacteria: Role in Disease*, checked
out January 20, 1929

—*Bacterial and Mycotic Infections of Man*,
checked out January 20, 1929

—*Basics of Pharmacology*, checked out
January 23, 1929

—*Diseases of the Lung*, checked out
February 2, 1929

—*Modern Advances in Treating Lung Disease*,
checked out February 2, 1929

—*Pulmonology Cures*, checked out
February 2, 1929

—*Anatomy and Physiology*, checked out
February 3, 1929

—The Blessing of Death, checked out
February 7, 1929

—Greeting Death with Peace and Dignity,
checked out February 7, 1929

—At Peace at Last: On Death & Dying, checked
out February 7, 1929

—Cunningham's Text-book of Anatomy,
checked out February 27, 1929

Eva pursed her lips. "So what does this tell us?"

"For the most part, these books are not only medical books; the topics get gradually more specific," Viviani said. "Look—they start out as general anatomy, and they move more specifically toward lung diseases."

Eva nodded, chin in hands. "Yeah, they do! And with the tuberculosis epidemic, we're likely looking for someone researching that, right?"

"Right." Viviani smiled. "You said it yourself, Eva: sometimes you have to look at things upside down to see them for what they truly are."

They were all thinking it, but it was Merit who finally said, "We don't think it was Lorena, do we?"

The girls shook their heads. "I really don't think so," Viviani said. "She told us she's afraid she'll miss her deadline on this piece because she can't find the information she needs. I think she's as frustrated as the rest of us that these books are missing. Maybe even more so."

"So what do we do next?" Eva said, fingertips drumming her cheekbones. "We can't exactly question everyone in the city who has tuberculosis."

Viviani thought about the library check-out cards sitting in a file folder in Miss Schneider's desk. "No." Viviani chewed her bottom lip, swirled a curl around her finger. "There's just something we're missing . . . ," she muttered. She looked at the photograph of the check-out cards they'd taken. "Let's go ask Miss Schneider if we can see those check-out cards again. We are *so close* to cracking this one. In fact, I feel all crackly just thinking about it!"

Merit twisted her gold hoop earring and pointed to the last few books on the list. "And we'd better hurry. It looks like our patient doesn't have much time."

CHAPTER THIRTY-TWO

Instinct,

Dewey Decimal 155.7

SEE ALSO: *behavior evolution, consciousness*

The Moppets raced across the hall to the administrative offices on the second floor. Viviani was breathless when the trio arrived at Miss Schneider's desk.

"Hello, Miss S! Do you think me and the Moppets could get another gander at those overdue check-out cards?"

And, Dear Friend, Miss Schneider smiled at what must've looked like three red-faced, panting sleuths, aglow with instinct and the knowledge that the answer to this riddle was at their very fingertips.

"Sure, girls." Miss Schneider opened a file and withdrew a stack of library check-out cards, about the size of a deck of playing cards. Each was scrawled with signatures, each signature with a date stamped next to the name.

Merit fanned the cards on Miss Schneider's small desk, and the four of them huddled over them. A nearby phone rang. "NYPL, how can I assist you?" an administrative worker sang. Typewriter keys clacked. Desk chairs squeaked. Viviani flipped the cards to and fro, but this space suddenly felt too hot and too tight, like a wool sweater shrunken in the wash.

"Can we take these out into the hallway, Miss Schneider?" Viviani asked.

Miss Schneider looked over her shoulder, at Mr. Bergquist's door. It remained closed. "I suppose. If I join you."

The Moppets plus one brought the stack of cards into the hallway, then lined them in a long row on the cool yellowy-pink marble. "Breathing room," Viviani whispered. "Okay, cards. Show us your secret."

Viviani ran her finger down each card and marveled at how different *Helen Hoogland* was from *Josef Goodman*. Signatures were fascinating—each a snowflake, each a thumbprint. Some signed with force and pressure. Some signed with grace and fluidity. *I really should study handwriting soon*, Viviani thought. *Talk about cracking amazing codes!*

Then, *focus!* she told herself. *Look closer* . . . She flipped the cards back and forth, back and forth . . .

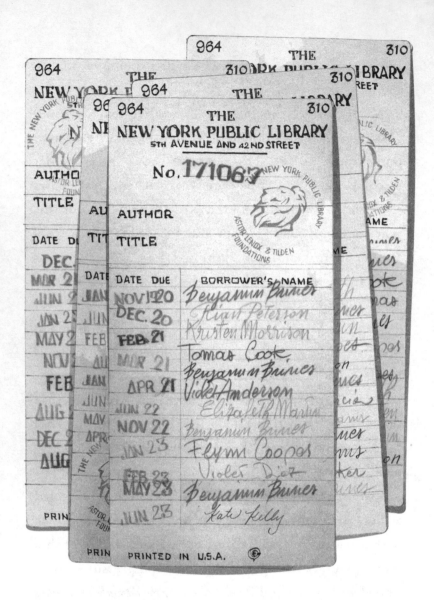

And she saw it. Right there, on the check-out cards,
was their story hoarder. "There you are."

Mr. Bergquist and Miss Schneider followed the Moppets to the address they had been given, on the Lower East Side.

"Forty-six, forty-eight, fifty—here it is! Number fifty-two!"

The apartment was below street level and had scrolly iron bars across the small window overlooking the cracked sidewalk. The book detectives crept down the steps, and Viviani and the girls crowded in behind them.

"Are you sure we should be here?" Eva whispered, grabbing Viviani's elbow. "What if—what if this is dangerous? Shouldn't we just let Mr. Bergquist handle all this?"

Merit bit her bottom lip; she looked torn on what to do.

Viviani knew, though, that what Papa had said earlier—the culprit wasn't *dangerous*, he was *desperate*—was accurate. "We'll be okay," she said, knowing that was indeed true. She knew this story hoarder, after all.

Mr. Bergquist knocked. Flakes of peeling blue paint fluttered to the dirty welcome mat.

The door swung wide. The figure inside was murky, difficult to see in the shadows.

Viviani gulped, imagining a terrible band of Al Capone–like gangsters huddled inside. *But I know I'm correct. I know this fellow is nice.*

"Edouard?" said a voice from inside the dark apartment. The figure stepped forward, his huge buggy eyes widening behind his thick glasses.

"Hi, Benjamin," Viviani said. "Dr. Monroe gave us your address."

The young intern stepped into the sunlight. He looked over his shoulder, then shooed the Moppets gently backward, closing the door behind him. "You can't come in here."

Viviani nodded. "There's a contagious patient inside."

Mr. Bergquist unfolded his copy of the list of missing books and showed it to Benjamin. "We need to see your bookshelves, Mr. Brines."

Benjamin blinked. Shifted. "Why?"

Viviani began to feel itchy. "Just let them see your shelves, Benjamin. They'll be nice if you do."

Benjamin shook his head. "You can't spend time in there. My mom—she's . . ." His voice caught. "She's very sick."

"Let's bring your books out here, then," Mr. Bergquist said rather forcefully. "I need you to open that door, sir."

Mr. Bergquist and Miss Schneider went inside Benjamin's apartment (with much protesting from Benjamin) and brought out every single book from his shelf, piling them on the sidewalk.

The Moppets and the book detectives dug through the pile and found all the books on the list.

Viviani frowned at Benjamin, who wouldn't make eye contact with her. She toed through the other books, and—

"Hey!" she said, picking up a book she knew: *The Philosophy of Death*. "This is ours, too! It's not on the list, but it definitely belongs to the library." There, in the front, was the library's inky stamp:

Viviani flipped it to and fro in her hands. It was definitely the book she had helped Mr. Tuttle repair. Same frayed, rounded corners. Same soft, bent spine . . .

Viviani smiled and flipped the book open to page three. There it was!

"And this nick," Viviani said. She showed it to Mr. Bergquist and Miss Schneider. "Mr. Tuttle notches these pages to show he's repaired a book once already. He marks each book on page three. But this book— this one I cut myself. This one needs to come home, too."

Eva flung her arms around Viviani's neck. Merit joined in, wrapping her hug around both of them.

"You did it, Viv!" Eva said, smiling.

"No," Viviani replied. "*We* did it. The Moppets. Together."

Miss Schneider chuckled. "You told me you and your friends would find these books, Viviani. 'Mark my words,' you said." Miss Schneider ran her finger across the notch on page three. "You certainly marked these words!"

CHAPTER THIRTY-THREE

Battles,

Dewey Decimal 355.4

SEE ALSO: *strategy, wars and battles*

Benjamin looked surprised, but then his shoulders fell. "I can explain everything. I just need some fresh air. Let's go sit on the front stoop."

The three girls followed Benjamin to the wide stairs of the tall brownstone while Mr. Bergquist and Miss Schneider continued to check the rest of the books on the sidewalk for NYPL stamps and nicks on page three. Benjamin drooped to the stairs, took off his glasses, and rubbed his bloodshot eyes. Viviani sat next to him. The other two girls sat on lower steps, looking up, awaiting his story.

Benjamin toed his sneaker into a crack in the concrete, and he suddenly looked very young to Viviani.

Viviani sighed. "You should've returned those books, Benjamin."

"I know." Benjamin looked down. "It's just . . . my sister died two months ago."

"Oh, I'm sorry to hear that . . ." Viviani paused, then added slowly, "So that's why you've checked out all these books before. You were trying to cure her."

Benjamin nodded, almost violently. "And now it's my mother. She's—well . . ."

"Very sick," Merit finished for him. Viviani's heart felt heavy in her chest.

Benjamin's eyes filled with tears. He suddenly sat up straighter. "My mother's name is Camila. She moved here from Colombia with nothing more than a thin pair of shoes and a dream for me and my sister."

Viviani smiled. "My mama is from Colombia, too!"

Benjamin laughed and swiped at the tear that popped out of the corner of his eye. "Yeah? Something tells me our mamas might be pretty similar. My mother would fight a bear for her family."

Viviani laughed, thinking of her own mama and the fire that lit her up like no one else. "Yes!"

"Fought her whole life, my ma. She fought to get here, to America. She fought to find a job. She fought her boss for better pay for all the workers, better working conditions. She fought for the women's right to vote."

Viviani felt *her* eyes sting. "She sounds exactly like my

mama. Nothing gets Mama riled up more than her League of Women Voters meetings."

Benjamin smiled, but he didn't stop the tears from streaking down his cheeks. "She fought to get me a great education. She fought to pay for my medical school by working two jobs. But *this*? This terrible disease. This tuberculosis?"

Benjamin continued, voice shaking. "This fight she's not winning. We don't have a lot of money," he said, waving his hand at the crumbling apartment building, "So we can't pay for lots of doctor visits and expensive treatment. We can't pay for a visit to a sanatorium upstate, the one thing that would truly help her recover. I thought I could fight this one for her. I thought if I could study tuberculosis, study the cures, study the latest medicines, I could puzzle out a cheaper solution."

Tears toppled at a steady rate. "Those books helped so much with my sister. I was sure I was so close to curing her. So close . . ." His voice trailed off and he swallowed. He shifted, straightening again. "So this time, I checked them out under false names. I didn't return them. I was going to. I was always going to, no matter the . . . *outcome*. But it felt like giving up on a cure for my ma, to return them before she was better. It felt like giving up hope. So I held on to them. And I held on to hope that way."

Benjamin was truly sobbing now. "All those battles

she fought for me, and here I am, losing the one battle I'm fighting for her."

The Moppets looked at one another, stricken, unsure how to comfort Benjamin.

Eva and Merit linked their fingers together, then Eva reached up and took Viviani's hand. Viviani felt stronger now. She lightly touched Benjamin's shoulder. "I'm so sorry, Benjamin. We'll try to help."

Eva blinked back tears. "And one thing is certain: when the Moppets set their minds to something, *nothing* will stop them."

CHAPTER THIRTY-FOUR

Private Investigators,
Dewey Decimal 363.28

SEE ALSO: *detectives, criminal investigators*

"Viviani, this is very impressive investigative work," Mr. Bergquist said to her in the wide marble hallway outside his office. Benjamin had returned to the library with Viviani and the book detectives, and he sat inside Mr. Bergquist's office now, awaiting a barrage of questions. "Are you sure you don't want to come work for me in another, say, seven or eight years?" He grinned.

"No, sir," Viviani chuckled. "First, I'm going to be a writer."

Mr. Bergquist laughed. "Well, now. If your books ever go missing, you'll have the skills to chase them down."

Viviani smiled. "Yes, sir. I suppose so."

"His case is a compelling one," Mr. Bergquist said, scratching his chin. "Never seen one quite like it."

"He said once he had those books at home, he wasn't even sure if he *should* bring them back," Viviani told the investigator. "I mean, those tuberculosis germs are vicious. Maybe he did us a favor."

Mr. Bergquist shrugged. "He held on to some very important medical books, Viviani."

Dr. Anderson arrived, and the two men hustled inside the office.

Viviani wished Merit and Eva had been with her to hear how impressed Mr. Bergquist was with their detective work. She bounced on her toes, her pride palpable.

The Moppets had solved another case!

Dear Friend,

> *Would I have done something similar to what Benjamin did, if it were MY mama?*
>
> *Yes, I think I would.*
>
> *Is it all relative, then? (Ha! Relative... Mama...No pun intended.) What I mean is this: WHEN should we keep information to ourselves, and when should we share it? Spies and code-breakers have information so private they have to hide it from all others. But knowledge about*

medicines and cures—that should be as widely available as possible, shouldn't it? And like everything in the world, there are stages in between. Where does one stage end and the next begin, is what I'm wondering.

For a while I thought I had maybe stolen that story. When I was writing it, it felt like the story just appeared on the page, like invisible ink reappearing. So it made me question whether maybe I really had stolen the idea. The line between inspiration and cheating is a lot blurrier than I realized. But I never FELT like a thief. I felt like I was honoring the author Wanda Gág and her writing and illustrations. That was my intent, at least. Intent. There's that word again. A few months ago, Papa told me the difference between a liar and a storyteller is INTENT. Do you mean to harm or hurt? Then you're a liar. Do you mean to entertain or charm? Then you're a storyteller.

I truly don't think Benjamin intended to harm anyone by holding on to those books. Just like I never intended to steal a story idea.

Today's code is straight from the heart, Dear Friend. It is a number-substitution code (A=1, etc.), so pretty straightforward:

9 8-15-16-5 9 3-1-14 8-5-12-16 7-5-20
2-5-14-10-1-13-9-14 15-21-20 15-6
20-8-9-19 16-9-3-11-12-5!

CHAPTER THIRTY-FIVE

Intention,

Dewey Decimal 248.4

SEE ALSO: *fate and fatalism, conduct of life*

Viviani watched as Dr. Anderson scanned the pile of evidence against Benjamin the following morning. She gulped—she knew that file didn't share the tale of the Benjamin *she* knew, the one fighting to save his mother's life. When Dr. Anderson gently put the file folder aside, Viviani cleared her throat and stepped forward.

"Dr., uh, Anderson, sir?" Viviani said.

He turned to her, and his face slowly lifted into a small smile. "Viviani! I understand I have you and your friends to thank for catching our bad guy!"

Bad guy? "But, sir, he didn't actually steal anything. He just . . . kept our books?" As she was saying the words, she realized how unconvincing she sounded.

"Viviani, in my mind, those two are one and the same. I'm considering pressing charges against this young man. He practically stole those books."

Viviani's heart raced. Pressing charges? *Stole?* Viviani knew exactly what it felt like to be accused of stealing something when, in fact, the intent had been very different.

"Sir, can I have a moment of your time?"

Dr. Anderson nodded. "Certainly, Viviani. I owe you at least that. Come—let's take a walk."

Their footsteps echoed in the near silence of the vast second-floor hall. Dr. Anderson strolled through the hallways of the library every morning. He did so slowly, quietly, almost like a meditation.

"I think of this library as my home," Dr. Anderson said softly. "But ha! Look who I'm saying that to! Within these marble walls, behind these iron doors, lives one of the world's largest and most diverse pools of knowledge. Many people think of this building in terms of stone: the cornerstone laid in 1902, the final stone laid in 1911. A beautiful building, built block by block. But I think of this library in terms of *books*. The first book put into cir- culation on opening day, May 24, 1911. The eighty-five miles of books on shelves, awaiting their perfect reader. Millions of pages! Hundreds of millions of words! This library was actually built *book by book*, Viviani."

Viviani smiled at the thought.

"So when someone impairs our ability to share our

books, well, for me, that's the absolute worst harm they can do to this institution. It is our very soul."

Viviani's heart twisted. "Dr. Anderson, I'd like to tell you about Benjamin."

And so she did. As she and the library director wound their way through wide, cool, quiet hallways, Viviani told him why Benjamin had held on to those books long past their due dates. She told Dr. Anderson about how Benjamin's sister died only months ago and how his mother was sick now, too. Benjamin was desperate.

"Benjamin sees books as precious, too," Viviani said. "He sees them as the blocks that build knowledge, just like you. Please don't have him arrested."

Dr. Anderson scratched his chin and said, " 'So much benevolence as a man hath, so much life hath he.' "

Viviani must've looked confused, because Dr. Anderson smiled. "Ralph Waldo Emerson. Perhaps we can give him a bit of leniency. Thank you for sharing his story, Viviani. Stories certainly change things."

Yes! Stories *do* change things!

If millions of stars could twinkle inside a person's brain all at once, it happened to Viviani just then.

"Oh, thank you, Dr. Anderson!" And off she ran, to yet another storytelling emergency.

CHAPTER THIRTY-SIX

Feature Writing,
Dewey Decimal 808

SEE ALSO: *journalism—authorship*

"**S**top the presses!" Viviani shouted to Lorena Hickok across Bryant Park. "Boy, do I have a scoop for you!" They sat on a wooden bench just behind the library. Well, Lorena sat. Viviani was too zingy-excited to sit, so she paced and talked, talked and paced. The sky was a mix of bright blue and puffy gray-white clouds that threatened to dump a cold spring shower at any moment. Tulips and daffodils stretched skyward, and the air smelled like impending rain.

Lorena nodded as she listened to Viviani. "Yep. Yeah, I definitely see." She paused. "Are you sure you want to give up your story being in the *Times*, Viviani? It's really good, you know."

Viviani paused as she thought of the hundreds of

thousands of *Times* readers, including her papa, who would never read her essay in newsprint. She had wanted so desperately to prove herself a story collector. A story-*teller*. A writer. She'd thought the way to do that was to see her name, her words, in print.

But she now knew she'd been a writer all along.

"Yep. I'm sure."

Lorena nodded. "You know, Viviani, I think this story is better than the one I've been working on for so long. Research can only take you so far. Stories—they need a *face*, don't they? A human element?"

Viviani smiled. "That's what makes them worth reading."

Lorena stood to leave, and Viviani blurted, "I hope we can trust you with this story, Miss Hickock." She crossed her arms. "You said it yourself: space in the *New York Times* is very valuable. Can you . . . can you make sure this story is worth it?"

Lorena shook Viviani's hand firmly. "I'll take good care of your friend's story, Viviani. I promise."

The next day, a story and a photograph appeared on page two of the *New York Times*:

Hoarded Books to Gain Knowledge, Save Mother from Death
By Lorena Hickok

Benjamin Brines is the face of tuberculosis.

"Well, that's certainly not a distinction I care to have," says the mild-mannered man of 20. "I'd far rather be the face of the cure for tuberculosis."

Benjamin works for Dr. Louise Monroe by day and attends medical school by night. In the tight hours in between, he cares for his mother, Camila Brines, who is sick with the disease. And late last year, Benjamin lost his sister, Luciana, to tuberculosis. As of the last census, over 88,000 people in the United States have died from tuberculosis, also called consumption. That is 7.7 percent of all the deaths in this country.

"Luciana was young and vibrant, and she made the best bandeja paisa you ever tasted." Benjamin laughs, but his eyes shine with tears. "Her daughter is only three. She'll never know how wonderful her madre truly was."

And now, just months after burying his sibling, Benjamin is reliving the horror. His mother was diagnosed with tuberculosis eight weeks ago and has rapidly declined in health since.

"When she started coughing up blood, just like Luci? Well, that's when I took action."

Benjamin means he started borrowing

books from the New York Public Library. Which, in and of itself, is no crime. Not returning them? Well, that's another story.

"I thought I might beat the game of life," Benjamin says of his decision to hoard medical books from the shelves of the NYPL. "My sister's death, see, it cleaned out our savings. We simply don't have the funds to send Mama to a sanatorium, which is what she truly needs." Here, Benjamin Brines grows visibly shaken. "So I thought if I studied hard enough, did all the things those amazing books recommend, that I could save her. And you know what? She started improving.

"I kept those books because I needed that hope. I kept those books because I want to save my mother."

Over the past few weeks, the library tracked the missing books to Mr. Brines. Earlier this week, a special investigator from the library searched his home and found the books. Mr. Brines's questioning followed.

"If it is a crime to hoard knowledge," Mr. Brines admitted, "then I will plead guilty."

Viviani Joffre Fedeler, Merit Mubarak, and Eva Derian also contributed to this story.

Papa scooped up Viviani and flipped her upside down, holding her by her shins, so that her head dangled inches from the floor. Her hair swept the floorboards.

"My girl's name is in the *New York Times*!" he said, jiggling her. Viviani laughed so hard that tears sprang out of her eyes and ran into her hairline. She had been just as surprised as anyone that Lorena had included the Moppets' names in the story. "As a *writer*! Did you see that, Cornelia? I'm gonna shake all those ideas right out of her head, because she's got so many of 'em! The *New York Times*!"

Cornelia laughed. "Don't make her vomit, John."

Viviani let her arms droop as her papa spun her around, upside down. She got the hiccups but didn't care in the least. As Eva said, sometimes it takes turning things upside down to see them for what they are. Because *she*, Viviani Fedeler, was a writer.

CHAPTER THIRTY-SEVEN

Kindness,

Dewey Decimal 177.7

SEE ALSO: *conduct of life, humanitarianism*

"**V**iviani, you and your friends need to come to the *Times* offices!"

Viviani's family didn't have a telephone in their apartment, but Lorena had called the administrative offices of the library, and a staff member had tracked Viviani down. (She was found in the Periodical Reading Room, folding open every copy of the *New York Times* to their article.) (*Their* article! In the *NEW! YORK! TIMES!*)

The Moppets got there as quickly as they could. They ran into Benjamin in the lobby.

"Did Lorena call you, too?" he asked.

The trio of girls nodded.

The elevator ride to the third floor was silent, but

when the doors slid open, the sounds of telephones ringing and typewriters clacking and reporters shouting were like a symphony of story to Viviani.

Lorena was there, bouncing on her toes. She grabbed Benjamin by the elbow. "C'mon!"

They followed her to perhaps the messiest desk of them all. Atop a pile of papers and staplers and pens sat a paper bag. Lorena motioned to the bag with a flourish.

"Go on. Take a look."

Inside the bag were letters. All addressed to Benjamin Brines, care of Lorena Hickok, the *New York Times*. Letters from across town. Letters from Pennsylvania. Letters from Tennessee. One letter had even traveled all the way from Canada!

Benjamin opened the one on top, from Alabama. He scanned it. His eyes filled with tears, and he dropped into Lorena's chair. "Oh, my," he whispered.

"Is everything okay?" Eva asked.

Viviani gently took the letter from his hand and read it aloud:

Dear Mr. Brines,

I, too, lost a family member to tuberculosis. Terrible killer. I'm sorry for your loss. I've enclosed all the spare money I have—$2.40—to help your ma get the treatment she needs.

And sure enough, there were two one-dollar bills and some change in the bottom of the envelope.

Merit reached into the bag, pulled out another letter. "May I?" she asked Benjamin.

He nodded slowly, as if he were underwater. "Sure."

Hello from Vermont, Benjamin!

I was so moved by your story that I wanted to do whatever I could to help. It's not much, but $10.60 is enclosed.

Eva opened one next, from Kentucky:

Dear Ms. Hickok,

I can't stand to hear that someone can't afford the medical treatment they need. Please make sure Benjamin Brines gets this money for his ma. And no more taking out them books and not returning them, son! That there's not right.

Inside was a crisp twenty-dollar bill.

"Is this—*whole bag* filled with letters like this?" Benjamin asked, voice wavering.

Lorena nodded. "Yes. I think so."

After opening almost a hundred letters, the whole time Benjamin swinging from laughter to tears back to laughter, he had nearly half the money needed for medical expenses for his mother.

"She's going to get help," Benjamin whispered. "She's going to be well again! And all thanks to the kindness of strangers."

Viviani nodded. "And thanks to the power of a good story!"

Over the next few weeks, more money trickled in. A jar full of change from a local third-grade class. A dime taped to a notecard from a man in Peru. Even John Jr. and Edouard donated some of their chore money. And finally, a poorly typewritten letter came in that offered this:

> I enjoy reading updates on Benjamin
> Brines—thank you for keeping us
> updated on them donations, Miz ~~Hikok~~
> Hickok. I'm moved by the cindness of
> all them strangers. I been offered a
> lot of cindness lately too. I kin pay
> whatever's left of them medical bills.
> That money's doing me no good stuffed
> in my mattress anyways.

Viviani hugged herself as Lorena read the letter over the phone. Benjamin's mother would be treated!

CHAPTER THIRTY-EIGHT

Surprise,

Dewey Decimal 152.4

SEE ALSO: *emotions, adaptability*

Viviani was late to her next lesson with Mr. Green, and he scowled at her as she ran, shoes shuffling and sliding on the slick floor, around the corner of the map room.

"That girl's late," he grumbled.

"Sorry!" Viviani chirped, falling into a chair beside him. "I was just on the telephone with Lorena. Benjamin's mama got checked in to the sanatorium upstate, and she's finally getting the treatment she needs!"

Mr. Green's face shifted. "Yeah. Uh. I saw your name in that paper. Your papa's a mite proud." He fought a grin (which rather looked to Viviani like he was fighting gas bubbles). "Bet you think you're the bee's knees right about now."

Viviani playfully shoved Mr. Green's arm. "Listen to you! You sound just like a youngster."

Mr. Green shrugged, then composed his face back into a scowl. "I'm just glad that anonymous donor chipped in the rest of the money."

Viviani paused.

Sat up straight.

That story hadn't run yet; Lorena had told Viviani just minutes earlier that the story of the final anonymous donor would be in the next day's issue.

"Yeah, well," Viviani said, sliding her eyes at Mr. Green. "That money was just sitting in your mattress anyways."

Mr. Green cleared his throat, shifted in his seat. He denied nothing.

She leaned toward him. "Your reading and writing have really improved, Mr. Green. That letter you wrote was impressive! Are you sure you still need these lessons?"

Mr. Green scowled so deeply that Viviani thought his face might slide to the floor. But he turned and pulled something out of his satchel.

Millions of Cats.

He tapped the familiar orange, yellow, and black cover.

"Course I do. Now, let's read."

CHAPTER THIRTY-NINE

Presents,

Dewey Decimal 745.92

SEE ALSO: *gifts, crafts*

The following day was the warmest day of spring so far, and Viviani took her time getting home: she smelled sausages frying and listened to a three-piece jazz band busking on the street and ran her finger through the film of yellowy pollen and soot that coated the tall black lampposts. At last, she reached the corner of Fifth and Forty-Second. There stood . . .

"Benjamin!" Viviani said with a smile. "How's your mama?"

"Better." Benjamin grinned back. "Thank you for asking."

"What are you doing here?"

"Well, I can't exactly go in *there* anymore," Benjamin

said. He thrust his thumb over his shoulder at the lovely library. "Unfortunately. But I understand why. Luckily, they've decided not to press charges against me and label me a thief. Gave me a fine of ten dollars and sent me on my way. Once Dr. Anderson read that *Times* story . . ."

Benjamin got choked up, lost his voice. He cleared his throat, adjusted his glasses, and handed Viviani a parcel.

"Listen, it's not much. But I owe you my gratitude. Thank you for all you've done for me and my family."

"Presents!" Viviani squealed, bouncing on her toes. She ripped open the brown parcel paper, and—

"Oh! OH!"

It was a book whose cover read *"Millions of Stars* by Viviani Joffre Fedeler. Inspired by the children's story *Millions of Cats* by Wanda Gág."

It was a bound copy of Viviani's winning short story!

"I asked your mama what I should do to thank you. She suggested this, since you gave up your *Times* prize for me and my ma. I hope you don't mind . . ."

"Mind? Mind?! Oh, Benjamin, thank you!" She flung the book open, held it to her nose, and *snnniiiiiijffffff*ed. "It's perfect." She sighed. "It smells just right."

Benjamin laughed.

Viviani hugged him a quick thanks, then rushed inside the library to her family's apartment.

"Guys? Guys—come on! Follow me!"

Edouard, John Jr., and Mama all glanced at one another curiously but followed Viviani. One thing was certain, Dear Friend. The Fedelers could not resist following a vivaciously shouted "Follow me!"

In the library, Mama whistled the special family whistle they used to find Papa in the massive building: *Twee-TWEE! Twee-TWEE!* Soon, they heard the reply whistle: *Twee-TWEE! Twee-TWEE!*

Papa found them in Astor Hall on the first floor. He, too, followed when presented with a beckoning "Follow me!"

The Fedeler family followed Viviani through the door marked STAFF ONLY and into the seven-story bookstacks. They wound their way through the iron-and-paper maze to exactly the spot she and Papa had visited before: the aisle marked FICTION: FA–FI.

Viviani found the space—*her* space—and then pulled the book—*her* book—out from the waistband of her skirt.

"Oh, Viviani." Her mama sighed. "It's gorgeous. But honestly—in your skirt?"

John Jr. whistled long and low. "Wouldja get a load of that book? What a beaut!"

Edouard nodded. "It's great, Viv. Fact: I always knew we'd see your name on the cover of a book."

Papa beamed and beamed and beamed some more. He cracked the spine and read it aloud:

Millions of Stars
By Viviani Joffre Fedeler
Inspired by the children's story <u>Millions of Cats</u>
by Wanda Gág
Once upon a time there was a very gentle girl
and a very gutsy girl. They lived in New York City,
where the lights glittered all night. But the
gentle girl was still afraid. She was afraid of the dark.
"If only we could capture the stars!"
the very gentle girl sighed.
"The stars?" asked the very gutsy girl.
"Yes," said the very gentle girl. "I wouldn't be so afraid of
the night if I had stars in my pocket."
"Then I will capture stars for you, friend!"
And off went the very gutsy girl.
First she tried a ladder. But she wasn't able
to reach the stars with just a ladder.
Then she climbed to the rooftop of the very tip-tallest
skyscraper. But even then, the very gutsy girl couldn't
reach the stars.
She even tried flying in an airplane—
whoosh! whirr! whizz! went the propellers through the

highest earthly skies. But still, the very gutsy
girl was starless.
At last, she had an idea!
The very gutsy girl gathered a jar. And inside the jar she
gathered:
Hundreds of fireflies! Thousands of fireflies!
Millions and billions and trillions of fireflies!
The very gentle girl giggled at this gift, and her
smile lit up the room just as brightly as the billions
of fireflies.
"But we can't keep them inside a jar!"
sighed the very gentle girl.
"We can't?" asked the very gutsy girl.
"We cannot," said the very gentle girl. "How can they fly?
Oh, we must set them free!"
And so out they went, into the lush green grass
of the park, and screwed off the lid of the jar.
And when they opened the cool metal lid, out flew:
Hundreds of fireflies! Thousands of fireflies! Millions and
billions and trillions of fireflies!
And the very gentle girl giggled, and her smile
lit up the park just as brightly as the billions
of fireflies.
The dark thickened, and the very gentle girl grew scared
again. "If only I could light up the night!"
And the very gutsy girl gave her a mirror.
And the very gutsy girl gave her a tickle.

243

*And the very gentle girl giggled. And her smile lit
up the night.
And it was the very best light of them all.*

Papa, Mama, John Jr., and Edouard all applauded loudly while Viviani took deep, silly bows. At last, Papa said, "Well, what're you waiting for? Put it on the shelf!"

And so Viviani claimed her space on the shelf, with *Millions of Stars* by Viviani Joffre Fedeler.

CHAPTER FORTY

Smell,

Dewey Decimal 612.86

SEE ALSO: *essences and essential oils, odors*

Dear Friend,

I have a STORY! Sitting on a SHELF! In the NEW YORK PUBLIC LIBRARY!

I've been thinking a lot about stories lately, particularly what it means to share them, to savor them, and, well, to hold on to them so tightly, no one else can have them. My book, even though it's inspired by another, is unique, and special, and one of a kind. So it's RARE. And because it's rare, it's valuable. Not necessarily in terms of money—although sure, that's sometimes the case, too. No, I mean valuable in that it offers something unique to the world, something that no other story offers in the exact same way. Stories and ideas are valuable in this way. Free, yet valuable. The whole thing kinda makes my head spin!

I've decided that I'm going to get Merit's and Eva's stories bound, too, and see if they'd like to place them on the shelves in THEIR spots. Benjamin's mom wouldn't be in good health again if it weren't for their help.

Miss Schneider kept asking the Moppets if we'd like a job. She was teasing at first, until a true part-time gig presented itself: filing the evidence she and Mr. Bergquist collect. And Eva got the job! Now she works after school just across the hall from our apartment. John Jr. claimed that everyone who works for the library has a secret initiation: they must be "buried in books." Eva, always the good sport, let me, Merit, John Jr., Carroll Case, and Edouard build a coffin of books around her while she lay still, eyes closed, hands crossed over chest. If she'd been *clutching a lily, I would've checked that she was still breathing—she was THAT GOOD at lying still! We were *just about* to lay the final ency-clopedia across her solemn face, when Miss O'Conner found us. Boy, I think her screams are still echoing around these marble walls!*

Dear Friend, Dear Unique Friend, the one that holds my special, one-of-a-kind, valuable thoughts? The Moppets await their next case. Until then, I believe I'll smell the pages of my book ONE MORE TIME.

This code should be an easy one to anyone who knows me and my home well: 179.9!

Viviani reached above her head, pulled her book off the shelf for the hundredth time this week, and then *snnniiiiiijfffff*ed. Aaaaah.

Dear Friend, nothing beats the smell of stories.

Author's Note

Dewey Decimal 809.33

SEE ALSO: *authors, American; literature, modern*

Dear Friend,

Just as Viviani Fedeler was inspired by Wanda Gág's book *Millions of Cats*, this book, *The Story Seeker*, was inspired by other stories as well! (Stories tend to do that—ignite the imaginations of story collectors!) Not only did a girl named Viviani Fedeler actually live in the New York Public Library with her family, but a special investigator named G. William Bergquist worked there. His job was to track down rare books that were missing from the library.

Benjamin Brines did indeed remove rare texts from the New York Public Library. According to news reports, he took rare books from the library to try to educate himself so that he could earn more money to take care of his mother properly.

His story was featured in the nation's newspapers over several weeks in 1920, and readers throughout the United States followed along as Benjamin Brines was questioned.

He told the court his sister had passed away two years prior. When his mother fell ill as well, he thought he could "beat the game of life" using books from the library. He wrongly did not return the books, but when the NYPL heard his story, they generously agreed to forgo pressing charges (which they could have done), and instead fine him $10. (That is approximately $125 in today's dollars.)

"If it is a crime to steal knowledge," he told the court, "then I'll plead guilty."

It's odd now to think about books once being so valuable that the New York Public Library employed a full-time detective to track down lost and stolen items. But when you consider that this was decades before computers and the internet, it makes sense: books like the ones Mr. Brines used were often the *only place* in the nation where that information could be found. If those books went missing, those facts, those *cures*, went missing.

And speaking of facts: Lorena Hickok was indeed a well-known journalist of the time, but she worked as an Associated Press correspondent whose stories sometimes appeared in the *New York Times*, rather than as a full-time *Times* staffer. I wanted to include her in this role because she was talented and fascinating: she was a gifted reporter whose editor recognized her abilities and gave her assignments that were rarely offered to women in her time, covering topics like politics, sports, and the Lindbergh baby kidnapping. She was friends with Eleanor Roosevelt and eventually worked for the Roosevelt administration. She, like Viviani, was a true story collector.

As for the Fedeler children, they lived a childhood that many of us would long to experience: growing up in the most iconic public library in the United States! Many of the adventures recounted here (including John Jr.'s wild snowball story and Mr. Fedeler's boxing account) are stories the Fedelers shared with the *New York Times*.

Today the New York Public Library system is made up of ninety-two locations and serves more than eighteen million patrons each year, who visit from all around the world. It currently houses more than fifty-five million items. For more information about the NYPL, including photographs of the many world-famous rooms mentioned in this story, visit nypl.org.

My sincerest thanks to the staff of the New York Public Library, especially Matthew Kirby, executive assistant to the chief external relations officer, for answering my many questions about the history of the Stephen A.

Schwarzman Building (so named in 2008). Also thanks to Keith Glutting, manager of the library's Visitor Volunteer Program, and Carrie Welch, chief external relations officer. I appreciate your sharing of both passion and wisdom! My thanks, too, to Vanessa Spray, whose love of stories and the NYPL truly shines.

Thank you to the Henry Holt/Macmillan Children's team who so passionately believe in sharing these stories: Tiffany Liao, Morgan Rath, Allegra Green, Christian Trimmer, and Rich Deas. My heartfelt thanks to Iacopo Bruno for his beautiful artwork and to Josh Adams for his continued friendship and guidance. It takes a team effort to turn a story into a book, and I'm grateful to work with the best teams in publishing.

As all story collectors know, every tale has nuances. True story collectors like Viviani Fedeler know to look for the many points of view in a story, like Benjamin's, or else you risk making a judgment that isn't entirely accurate. Seek out as many versions of a story as you can, Dear Friend. It can only get you closer to the Truth of that story.

Codes and Code Breaking

Dear Friend,

Did you crack Viviani's codes within her captain's log? Here are their answers:

Page 97, in Morse code: "The story hoarder is hiding someone's cure!"

Page 103, in the Caesar Shift: "Stories are missing everywhere! I'll find you, words, I promise."

Page 109, Edouard's Typewriter Code: "I will find you, missing stories."

Page 180, using symbols for letters: "Did I do it? Did I steal that story idea?"

Page 224, the number-substitution code: "I hope I can help get Benjamin out of this pickle!"

Page 247: That is the Dewey Decimal number for "Gratitude. See also: *joy*." Dewey Decimal numbers are also a code!

Codes are indeed older than human language, and their history is fascinating. Codes range from animals communicating with one another to Caesar instructing his large armies, to the brave and amazing Choctaw, Navajo, and Comanche code talkers during the two world wars, all the way to their modern usage in computer programming. Codes are a way to communicate secretly, so their story is often entangled in tales of spies and battles and undercover operations. One code that was developed in Viviani's era and used by the Germans in the Great War (now referred to as World War I) was known as ADFGX. Here's how it works:

	A	D	F	G	X
A	a	b	c	d	e
D	f	g	h	i/j	k
F	l	m	n	o	p
G	q	r	s	t	u
X	v	w	x	y	z

Every letter used in a message becomes a combination of two letters, all using A, D, F, G, and X. Find the letter on the grid above, then use a combination of those five letters to spell the word. For example, *Hello* would be DFAXFAFAFG. Can you see how? This might seem fairly straightforward, but in wartime the letters within the grid were often scrambled (in other words, not in alphabetical order as they are here). Once that occurred, this became a very hard code for enemies to crack without the key!

One of the coolest things about a good code is that it can be simple, but as long as only you and the recipient know the key, it can be a challenge for others to decipher. Try coming up with a code of your own! Maybe you could substitute emojis for letters, or develop a grid like the one above but with numbers. The possibilities are endless!

To learn more about codes, head to your local library and check out more books on the subject, including *The Top Secret History of Codes and Codebreaking* by Roy Apps, and *Top Secret: A Handbook of Codes, Ciphers, and Secret Writing* by Paul B. Janeczko and Jenna LaReau.

AFFGAGAXGF AAGDAX AFFGFGFA, AGAXAAGD DAGDDGAXFFAG!